Jorge Icaza

Huasipungo

A NOVEL

THE VILLAGERS

Authorized Translation and Introduction by
BERNARD M. DULSEY

Foreword by J. CARY DAVIS

Southern Illinois University Press CARBONDALE AND EDWARDSVILLE
Feffer & Simons, Inc. LONDON AND AMSTERDAM

Library of Congress Cataloging in Publication Data

Icaza, Jorge, 1906–
  Huasipungo.
  (Arcturus books, AB118)
  Original ed. issued in series: Contemporary Latin
American classics.
    I. Title. II. Title: The villagers.
[PZ3.I177Hu8] [PQ8219.I2]   863   73–9551
ISBN 0–8093–0653–0
98 97 96 95   11 10 9 8

AR CT
UR US
BOOKS ®

Copyright © 1964 by Southern Illinois University Press
All rights reserved
Arcturus Books Edition September 1973

This edition printed by offset lithography
  in the United States of America
Designed by Andor Braun

Foreword

J. CARY DAVIS

WE ARE PROUD and honored to inaugurate our new series of
Contemporary Latin American Classics with this, the first
authorized English translation of Jorge Icaza's *Huasipungo*.
It may seem strange that this great novel of social protest, depicting the exploitation of the Indian in Ecuador—
published in 1934 and translated in rapid succession into
almost a dozen languages of Europe and the Orient—should
have had to wait so long to appear in English. A generation
of American readers which has been brought up on Heming-
way, Steinbeck, and Faulkner will welcome this addition to
the wealth of literature now available in translation. The
title chosen for this edition, *The Villagers*, was thought to
convey most adequately the essential meaning of the original
Quechuan term *Huasipungo* used by the author.

The translator, Bernard M. Dulsey of the University of
Kansas City, is himself the author of numerous scholarly
articles in the field of Spanish language and literature, ap-
pearing in such journals as *Hispania, Hispanófila, The
Modern Language Journal*, and others. He is the prose fiction
editor for Peru, Ecuador, and Colombia for the *Handbook of
Latin American Studies*, a yearly publication of the Library
of Congress. He is also associate editor of the University of
Kansas City *Review*. Professor Dulsey was born in Chicago
in 1914, received his A.M. from the University of Chicago
(1939) and Ph.D. from the University of Illinois (1950) in
Spanish studies. He served in the U.S. Army in World
War II, rising from private to second lieutenant in three
years. Dulsey has been visiting professor of Spanish in sum-

mer quarters at a number of American universities, as well as in San Miguel de Allende, Gto., Mexico. He began his college teaching in DePauw University in 1941, and moved from Purdue University in 1951 to the University of Kansas City, where he is now Professor of Spanish.

Professor Dulsey has had wide experience traveling and studying in Latin America and Spain, and has made the acquaintance of many of the outstanding writers in these countries. As a good friend of Icaza's and conversant with every aspect of that author's life and works, he is uniquely qualified to interpret to the American public the novelist's message in all its essential characteristics. A great deal of meticulous labor has gone into this task to insure accuracy. Professor Dulsey has carefully checked with señor Icaza each expression that seemed to have a special regional use or connotation, in an effort to convey the author's true intent.

It seems fitting that Icaza's first novel to be made widely known to the English-speaking world should thus be presented as a co-operative venture in scholarship, on the part of (1) the author himself, one of the outstanding intellectuals in South America and the Hispanic world, (2) the translator, an eminent American scholar and professor of languages in this country, and (3) Southern Illinois University Press, which is greatly concerned with publishing works which have vital meaning for this day and age, and impact upon our modern times.

Southern Illinois University
August 10, 1963

Preface

JORGE ICAZA

EVER SINCE 1934, the date of its first publication in Quito, *Huasipungo*, a short novel of Ecuadorian social reality, has hoped and—why not admit it?—has desired with all the eagerness of embarking on a bold adventure to be translated and published in the language of Herman Melville, Mark Twain, Walt Whitman, and Edgar Allan Poe. It was then its hope to pound at the doors of the great cities of the North with a deep emotional impact: a bold Hispano-American denunciation in a logical fraternal extension. This so it could participate in the biblical pilgrimage—its experience in other latitudes: pilgrimages into the Portuguese, French, German, Italian, Czech, Swedish, Polish, Hungarian, Servo-Croatian, Russian, etc.—through the byways of a self-centered existence which perhaps had forgotten other people's sorrows, as a cry for justice, for equilibrium, for harmony, to reach ultimately the curious ears of the rural masses and to tell them in a low voice of the harsh struggle of the man of the Andean plateaus and of the tropical jungle, a dialogue which is interwoven with a similarity of efforts and a common ardor of rebellion; and, finally, it was its hope to offer testimony of a subhuman existence in the very heart of a period of social reforms and of incredible conquests of space.

In spite of a series of obstacles, conflicting personal interests, fears, and prejudices, the time for *Huasipungo's* bold adventure is now at hand. It has arrived thanks to the deep humanist feeling, the moral quality, and the singular talent of my friend, Professor Bernard Dulsey, who, while traversing these Southern lands, has learned to understand

and to feel the essential and existential truth of the Hispano-American countries. He has succeeded, likewise, in distinguishing where lay the reactionary falseness of the political bosses, landowners, military leaders, and oligarchs wearing masks of heroism, holiness, knowledge, and sacrifice, and whence emanated the authentic creative, cultural, and emotional force of the great city and rural majorities.

The particular, regional conscience of *Huasipungo* since the moment of its conception has sought to stimulate the courage and hopes of the Indian, of the coastal rustics, of the half-breeds, of the peasants, and of all the humble folks of the Ecuadorian land. But the spirit of its sincerity has found common suffering in every latitude, injustice on all shores, which is the reason—its origin, its trajectory, and its destiny —that this book when it reaches the English-language reader will seek, as always, the preference, understanding, love, and communication of those who nourish the world's body and spirit by sprinkling their fruitful sweat on our Mother Earth.

Quito, Ecuador
May 27, 1963

Introduction

BERNARD M. DULSEY

JORGE ICAZA, now fifty-seven years old and Ecuador's finest novelist, is in the not too unusual position of being more respected abroad than he is at home.[1] The opposition in his homeland takes two positions, completely removed from each other yet completely in accord in their disapproval of Icaza.

Those in the first camp have denied (and still deny) that Icaza's picture of the Indian problem, as mirrored in *Huasipungo* and his other works, is a true one.[2] They charge that Icaza used his fantasy overmuch; that he deliberately distorted facts in order to make a "shocking" novel; and that

1. Most of the material presented in this introduction is based on my article, "Jorge Icaza and His Ecuador," in the *Hispania* of March, 1961.

2. It must be noted here that the original version of *Huasipungo* is not the one presented here in translation. It is based on the author's own revision of September, 1953. Icaza himself requested that I make my translation from the expanded 1953 version which he considers superior to his original work.

By 1934, the first appearance of his internationally-known *Huasipungo*, Icaza had already published six works for the theatre: *El intruso*, 1929; *La comedia sin nombre*, 1930; *Por el viejo*, 1931; *¿Cuál es?*, 1931; *Como ellos quieren*, 1932; and *Sin sentido*, 1932. In 1933 a book of short stories, *Barro de la sierra*, revealed a story-telling talent which ripened fully a year later in his first and greatest novel, *Huasipungo*. In 1935 his second novel, *En las calles*, won the national literature award in Ecuador. Since then he has published *Flagelo*, a drama, in 1936; *Cholos*, a novel, in 1937; *Media vida deslumbrados*, a novel, in 1942; and *Huairapamushcas*, another novel, in 1948. In 1952 his collection of six shockingly violent tales of death appeared under the title of *Seis veces la muerte*. His latest work to date is the novel *El chulla Romero y Flores*, published in 1958.

he really had little firsthand knowledge of the Indian. To them Icaza is a fraud.

The second group argues that perhaps Icaza is accurate in his description of the Indian problem; but, they add, such miserable conditions, even when they truly pertain, do not justify their inclusion in "literature." In other words Icaza should not have been so disgustingly forthright in his presentation of the problem. Such things are not pretty to read.

But *Huasipungo*, a grim tale of misery and despair, is not devoid of poetry. There is much unusual imagery in the Spanish, which I have made every effort to preserve in the English version. Startling descriptions of man and nature frequently occur. Abundant evidence of poetry can be found, for example, in the description of the village of Tomachi, of the great storm, of the flood, and in Andrés' lament for Cunshi.

Reading Icaza is a profoundly moving and deadly serious experience. There is practically no humor; but why expect humor from an author whose self-imposed task it has been to reflect accurately the life of the Indian and that of the underprivileged half-breed? Most of the serious *indianista* novelists use their books as formidable weapons in a ceaseless combat against the misery of the lower classes. In Ecuador these include much more than half the population.

One of Icaza's outstanding merits is his capacity to synthesize his material. His novels are short, yet complete. The reader does not feel defrauded at the end of the novel; for his protagonists, although sketched in verbal *goyescas*, are nearly always flesh and blood. The conditions portrayed in his works still largely obtain, as any recent visitor to Ecuador can testify. Even in the last decade there have been advertisements in Ecuadorian newspapers for the sale of haciendas with the peons included! And in certain mountain areas the infant mortality rate is still 50 per cent.

There has been a natural tendency in the United States to compare Icaza with the Steinbeck of *Grapes of Wrath*. But while *Huasipungo* and *Grapes of Wrath* are both products of the "thirties" there are now apparent two vital differences: first, the percentage of "Okies" in the United States was very much smaller than that of the *huasipungueros* in Ecuador; and second, the "Okies" are no longer a problem.

Here are Icaza's own unhappy words about the effect of his most famous novel. In an interview in 1959 he stated: "I had the illusion that *Huasipungo*, with its tremendous protest . . . would help to redeem the *huasipunguero*. Help to make him known in his sorrow, in his loneliness, and in his despair. The Indian in Ecuador still lives in the same situation. *Huasipungo*'s message is absolutely pertinent even now. . . . It is my great literary success but it has also been my bitter disappointment, somewhat like the shattering of a dream." [3]

Adrian Villagómez L., writing in *Excelsior*, quotes Icaza on the sources for his *Huasipungo:* "Among them, the awakening with my eyes focused on our reality, the study of experiences undergone in the postwar years of the first World War; some ideas from the Russian revolution, and especially the scientific advances of the epoch." [4] Icaza believes that the value of his novel has been "to have presented in a frank and sincere manner our peasants' social problems before all of Latin America." Of the lesson to be learned from the novel Icaza said, "*Huasipungo*'s solution is that an instinctive rebellion has to be wisely led and directed or else it will surely fail."

Icaza has his own ideas about what makes literature and where it should seek its subject matter. "I don't believe in differences between so-called social literature and literature purely for its own sake. I do believe it has long been our error, here in America, to look too much toward Europe, to imitate their artists and their problems when here at home we have had such brutal and fascinating raw material to work with. We shall succeed in obtaining true universality looking toward America, not letting ourselves be tugged along by Europe." [5]

3. From an interview, "Diez minutos con Jorge Icaza," by Martín Alberto Noel in the literary supplement of *Clarin* of Buenos Aires, July 26, 1959.
4. From the *Excelsior* of Mexico City, February 15, 1960.
5. Martín Alberto Noel, *op. cit.*

Like Azuela, the great novelist of the Mexican revolution, with whom he may very fairly be compared, Icaza obtains great verisimilitude by accurately mirroring the customs, beliefs, and even the very speech of his characters. Their speech is larded with Quechuan terms which often raise linguistic obstacles for the North American reader of Spanish. Both Icaza and Azuela have written novels, not for personal profit and prestige, but simply because social, political, and economic injustices aroused their deep compassion. They wrote because something deep within them impelled them to write. Azuela was a physician. Icaza presently runs a bookstore in downtown Quito. The sad truth is that the finest writers in the Spanish language, almost without exception, must make their living in some other pursuit.

Let us examine the Ecuadorians through the eyes and novels of Jorge Icaza. In his works the Indians and half-breeds usually share the same character deficiency—an inability to base their thoughts and actions on anything beyond their *immediate* personal needs or problems. Thus there is no cohesion or unity among the downtrodden even though they form the majority of the nation. According to the author, the very few Indians who show leadership qualities are suborned or ruthlessly removed from the arena by the forces of the status quo. Astute half-breeds may obtain petty power, but when they do they then seem to do their best to forget the Indian side of their heritage.

Icaza frequently dwells on the inferiority complex of the half-breed or mulatto. In his latest novel, *El chulla Romero y Flores*, the protagonist suffers continual anguish because of his mixed white and Indian blood. He imagines himself superior because of his father's blood and degraded through his mother's Indian heritage. Only at the end of the book does he realize that he "belongs" to his own cholo group and that he has slim chance of happiness or of material success if he tries to intrude on the white man's world. Icaza has undoubtedly been denounced by some of his countrymen for indicating that the cholo, as well as the Indian, is discriminated against in Quito; and that it may be better for the cholo (certainly better for his peace of mind) to live in poverty in harmony with his peers than to battle to pull himself up the social ladder to a world not really his.

Addiction to drink is a common vice in Ecuador. The peon or campesino throughout Latin America wrestles with this mighty enemy. Alcoholism may cost him his livelihood or even his very life as the result of a drunken brawl. The illiterate peon (almost a redundant expression) who drinks, usually to forget his misery, pain, hunger, or unemployment, finds himself mired ever deeper in the depths of despair, if not of crime itself. Alcohol thus creates the most vicious of circles.

The bureaucrats of Ecuador take full advantage of this weakness in the Indian, and on election day they insure their "election" through this vice. They get the Indians drunk in their native villages—the alcohol is free that day, and more is promised—and then cart them by bus or truck to the nearest city, where the inebriates are told how to vote. This practice has been observed in Mexico even in recent years and it is still noted in the predominantly Indian countries of Central and South America. In Icaza's *En las calles* (1935) this travesty of justice is graphically described.

Icaza is quite unhappy with the church in Ecuador. Its importance in Ecuadorian life is paradoxical. Officially there is, as in Mexico, a legal separation of church and state. But the anticlerical statements, which abound in Mexico, are not so popular in Ecuador. On the contrary, the church in Ecuador is strongly entrenched. When asked his opinion of the church Icaza told me, "Religion has had a negative influence." He went on to say that there is a good deal of paganism in the church liturgies in Ecuador. But notwithstanding the vicious priest he portrays in *Huasipungo*, Icaza, it must be pointed out, is much more against clerical abuses and hypocrisy than he is against the tenets of the church.

Icaza's landowners and government officials usually have their price. For the petty officials the price is not high, but it is far beyond the emaciated purse of the Indian. It must also be remembered that Icaza's Indians are far from being models of virtue themselves; they are only human. Often they resort to petty crimes to stay alive. Their women are often forced into prostitution or concubinage in order to exist. They are not the "noble" Indians of the European and American Romanticists but the real Andean Indians of today in all their unwashed misery. They suffer from malnutrition, alcoholism, superstition, and ignorance.

And so, as in the novels of the Peruvian Ciro Alegría a few years later, we find the Indians in a ceaseless combat with hunger and oppression. This unrelenting battle deadens their social sense and even when finally goaded into some concerted action they are usually just a leaderless mob.

Is Icaza then always pessimistic? If we adhere to the dictionary definition strictly we can safely say he is not. Inasmuch as the life he portrays is so realistically detailed some readers would classify him as a pessimist for this alone. But actually a pessimist is one who consistently looks on the hopeless side of life. Icaza is, after all, essentially a propagandist, a reformer, an artist, an intellectual who strives through his writings to improve the political and socioeconomic status of the lower classes.

Would it not therefore be equally just to label Icaza a hopeful man who seeks to better the lot of his country by a ruthless exposé of its festering sores and gaping wounds? For to recognize that a sick man is sick is logically the first step necessary to make him well again. To maintain that someone sick is whole is not being optimistic; it merely indicates an unforgivable stupidity or acute myopia in the examining physician.

Icaza is not pro-Indian only; he is much more. He is pro-justice, for equal justice and opportunity for all his countrymen, regardless of their poverty or the color of their skins.

Racial prejudice does exist in much of the Latin American world; it is not solely the possession of the English-speaking nations, as some would have us believe. In a review of Icaza's latest novel, *El chulla Romero y Flores* (1958), the Argentine critic Valentín de Pedro says:

All this means that racial prejudice has not been eradicated from Hispano-American society, that it still persists, especially in those countries which have a considerable percentage of Indian population, such as Ecuador.[6]

It is not necessary to be an acute observer to note how the political and economic conditions today in Ecuador parallel those of Mexico in 1910. But as yet no Madero has appeared to help uplift the submerged masses in present-day Ecuador. The real Ecuadorian revolution is yet to come, but Icaza's novels foreshadow it as surely as Azuela's early novels foreshadowed and justified the Mexican revolution. I do not mean that the Ecuadorian revolution must necessarily follow the bloody Mexican pattern but it *must* entail a drastic change in the social and political thinking of the governing minority.

The final responsibility for the accuracy and fidelity of the translation is, of course, completely my own. But, as usual in such cases, I have had several very able people abetting me in my efforts.

I wish to express my thanks particularly to the author for his unstinting co-operation during three years of constant correspondence in which he answered my countless questions on regional vocabulary and other pertinent matters. In the work of translation itself, my wife Elaine contributed many worthwhile suggestions. As she says, *Huasipungo* was a part of the family for two years! My warmest thanks go to my friend and colleague, Dr. William Ryan, to Dr. J. Cary Davis with whom I also maintained an unflagging correspondence concerning the translation, and finally, to editor Vernon A. Sternberg of the Southern Illinois University Press for the painstaking care with which he readied this manuscript for publication.

San Miguel de Allende, Mexico
June 24, 1963

6. Valentín de Pedro, in his review of *El chulla Romero y Flores* in *La Prensa* of Buenos Aires, June 5, 1959.

The Villagers

HUASIPUNGO

THE DAY GREETED Alfonso Pereira with enormous contradictions. He had just left in the hands of his wife and daughter, and to their women's intuition and instinct, the unresolved problem of "honor at stake," as he called it. As usual in a situation like this—from which *he* had to emerge blameless—he had banged the door on his way out, muttering a series of oaths under his breath. His cheeks, normally rosy and glowing with Andean sunshine and the tangy mountain air, had taken on a sickly hue. But the street scenes gradually appeased his bile and restored his normal color.

"No. It can't go on like this. I can't let the thoughtless act of an innocent seventeen-year-old girl, deceived by a scoundrel, a criminal, bring dishonor to us all."

"Me, a gentleman of high society . . . My wife, a pillar of the church . . . My family name . . . ," thought Don Alfonso, looking at, but not seeing, the people who were passing him, who were bumping into him. Helpful ideas, which can hide anything and can skillfully and decently disguise everything, could not be summoned by his brain. His poor brain. Why? Ah! Because they were being throttled in his fists, in his throat.

"Son-of-a-bitch."

The thought of his debts contributed to his ill humor: debts to his uncle, Julio Pereira, to the archbishop, to the banks, to the national treasury for taxes on income, on real estate, on the home, to the town for . . . "Taxes. Goddam taxes. Who can pay them? Who? My money! Five thousand . . . eight thousand . . . the interest . . . Money doesn't come that easy. Nooo . . . ," Don Alfonso said to himself while he was crossing the street, absorbed by that problem which had become a mocking phantom to him. "Does money grow on trees? Does it rain on the virtuous like manna from heaven? Oh! . . ." The onrush of a streamlined car, costly as a house, and the sound of the horn and the brakes rudely shook his worries from him. On the edge of that cold, bottomless pause which is caused by the fright of a peril miraculously avoided, Don Alfonso Pereira noticed a friendly hand summoning him from the interior of the vehicle which had almost erased him from the gray page of the street with its tires. Who could it be? Perhaps an apology? Perhaps some request? The unknown then stuck his head out of the car window and ordered him in a familiar voice:

"Come. Get in."

It was fate, it was his biggest creditor, it was his uncle Julio. He had to obey, had to approach, had to smile.

"How . . . ? How are you, uncle?"

"I almost flattened you, *but good*."

"That doesn't matter. Since it was you . . ."

"Get in. We've got to speak of some very important things."

"Delighted," said Don Alfonso, climbing into the car with a feigned pleasure and then seating himself next to his powerful relative. His uncle was a bulky figure with bushy eyebrows, grayish hair, challenging look, deep wrinkles, and dry, pallid lips. He had a mania for using "we" as if he were a department store clerk or a member of some secret gang.

The subject of conversation of the two gentleman became interesting and candid only when they reached the private office of the elder Pereira, an office with a frosted glass door, furnished with a huge desk which groaned under the weight of hundreds of papers and dossiers. There were also olive-green filing cabinets in the corners, ample divans which comfortably swallowed the victims of the multiple wheelings and dealings of a landowner's shrewdness, and a huge painting of the Sacred Heart of Jesus by a certain Mideros. There was also an old wooden coatrack, an anachronism in that luxurious retreat of modern style, which, as one could imagine, served to hang up one's jokes and smiles along with hats and the crestfallen umbrellas.

"Well, now, . . . My dear nephew."

"*Sí.*"

"Three weeks ago . . ."

"One of the promissory notes came due . . . the largest one . . . ," concluded Don Alfonso mentally, shaken by a shiver of anxiety and uncertainty. But the old man, without his usual stern mien and with a spark of hope in his eyes, went on:

"It's more than twenty days. You're ten thousand sucres overdrawn. I haven't wanted to press you because . . ."

"Because . . ."

"Well, because we have in our grasp an opportunity that will make us all millionaires."

"Ha . . . Ha . . . Ha . . ."

"Sí, hombre. First you ought to know that we have gone on an exploratory trip to your hacienda at Cuchitambo."

"Exploratory?"

"What a Godforsaken place! It hurts to see it."

"My business affair here . . ."

"Here! It's time for you to consider it seriously," said the old man in a fatherly tone.

"Oh!"

"Perhaps my suggestions and those of Mr. Chapy could save you!"

"Mr. Chapy?"

"He's the one in charge of the development of Ecuadorian timber. A gentleman of great means, of extraordinary promise, and with millionaire connections abroad. One of those *gringos* who can push the world around with the tip of his finger."

"A *gringo*," repeated Don Alfonso, dazzled with surprise and hope.

"On the survey we made with him through your property we took a quick look at your forests and we found five excellent woods: arrayán, motilón, canela negra, huilmo, and panza."

"Ah! And so?"

"We've got enough to supply ties for all the railways in the republic. And still some left for export."

"Export?"

"I understand your surprise. But that isn't the most important thing. Not at all. I believe the gringo has sniffed oil in that area. A month ago, more or less, El Día had a very important article about how rich in petroleum the eastern ranges are. It compared them with the oil-rich lands of Baku. I don't know where that is but that's what the newspaper said."

Don Alfonso, in spite of feeling a little disconcerted, nodded his head as if he really understood the affair.

"It's very promising for us. Especially for you. Mr. Chapy is offering to bring in machinery neither you nor I could ever afford. But for good reasons, and here I agree completely with him, he will do absolutely nothing, nothing at all, until he is sure that the necessary improvements will be made on your hacienda, which is the principal strategic point of the entire area."

"Oh! Then . . . I'll have to make improvements?"

"Of course! A good road is needed."

"Across the swampy part of your hacienda and from the town. It's not so long."

"Several kilometers."

"Disadvantages! You're always raising obstacles!" shrieked the old man, his face hardening.

"No. It's not that."

"He also demands a few things that I believe are easier and less important. The purchase of the Filocorrales and Guamaní forests. And, oh, yes, you'll have to clear out all the native huts—the huasipungos—along both banks of the river. Undoubtedly so the developers can build homes there."

"But to do this overnight?" murmured Don Alfonso, harassed by the many problems that he would have to solve in the future. He, who as an authentic landowner—a patrón grande, su mercé—had always allowed things to appear and fall into his grasp by the work and grace of the Almighty Father.

"He's not giving you a deadline. Whatever time you need."

"And the money for . . . ?"

"That's my affair. I'll help you. We'll form a corporation. A small one."

That was more convincing, more protection for the clear-thinking landowner who, with a nervous grin, dared to ask:

"You?"

"Sí, hombre. A job like this seems hard for you

because you are used to accepting without complaint whatever the administrators of your estate or the caretakers of your property feel like sending you: a pittance."

"That may be . . ."

"The consequences are quite apparent. Your fortune is going to pot. You're almost bankrupt."

Unable to find a pretext to avoid the gaze of his good uncle, Don Alfonso Pereira could only wave his arms like a man persecuted by a relentless destiny.

"No, don't do that. You must understand that this is no time to show cowardice or despair."

"But you believe that I've got to go and do these things myself."

"Who else? The blessed angels?"

"Oh! And with these good-for-nothing Indians."

"There are many resources in the country and in the towns. You know that very well."

"Yes, I know. But you mustn't forget that those people are annoying and lazy, full of superstition and mistrust."

"*That* we'd be able to take advantage of."

"Besides . . . that clearing out the huasipungos . . ."

"What about it?"

"The Indians become very deeply attached to that small plot of land which is leased to them in return for their work on the hacienda. Even worse than that, in their ignorance they think they own it. You know that. On it they grow a few things and raise their animals."

"You're overly sentimental. We've got to conquer all obstacles, no matter how big. The Indians . . . so what? What are those Indians to us? Or rather . . . They should concern us . . . of course . . . They can be an extremely important factor in the whole business. The workers . . . The labor . . ."

The questions which had habitually peeped out of the crevice of the subconscious mind of the younger Pereira—"Does money grow on trees? Does it rain on the virtuous like manna from heaven? Where am I going to get the money to pay the taxes?"—disappeared before the solution, the . . .

"Yes, it's so. But Cuchitambo has too few Indians for such a huge task."

"With the money that we'll supply you, you can buy the Filocorrales and Guamaní forests. The Indians come with the forests. All rural lands are bought or sold with their peones."

"That's true."

"Hundreds of Indians who can serve you well by building the road. What do you say now?"

"Nothing."

"What do you mean, nothing?"

"I mean that, in the first . . . place . . ."

"And in conclusion, too. Otherwise . . . ," finished the old man, brandishing like a deadly sword some papers which were doubtless the I.O.U.'s and the past-due notes of his nephew.

"Sí. O.K. . . ."

As he left his uncle's office, Don Alfonso Pereira felt a bitter taste in his mouth, a taste of repressed fury, a desire to curse, to kill. But as he went along the street and remembered that in his home he had still some unresolved problems, shameful ones, all the despondency caused by the Cuchitambo affair slowly evaporated. Yes. It evaporated through the hole of his punctured honor. The callowness and passion of a daughter inexpert in the deceits of love were to blame. "The little fool. My duty as a father. I would never permit her to marry a half-breed—a cholo. Cholo, body and soul. Besides . . . the wretch has disappeared. Son-of-a-bitch. His name was

Cumba . . . Uncle Julio is right, quite right. I ought to get into that big deal with . . . the gringos. Trustworthy people. They're always our saviors. They'll give me money. The money is the main thing. And . . . of course . . . why didn't I see it before? I'm a stupid fool. I'll bury the poor girl's shame on the hacienda. Wait till I get a hold of that goddam Indian . . . My wife can still . . . Can make people think . . . Why not! And Santa Ana? And the families that we know? Oo-oo-oo . . . ," he said to himself with all the emotion and mystery of a romantic novel. He then quickened his pace.

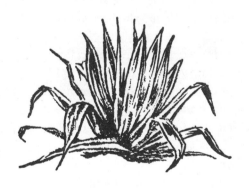

IN A FEW WEEKS Don Alfonso Pereira, forced by circumstances, settled his accounts and signed papers with his uncle and Mr. Chapy. And one morning at the end of April he left Quito with his family, his wife and daughter. Neither their relatives nor their friends, nor the prudish women of Quito high society even dared to doubt the economic motivation that was forcing such distinguished personages to leave the capital. The Southern railway, a narrow-gauge railroad, with a plume of nauseating smoke, a rain of fiery sparks, and a whistle of doleful complaint, brought them to a tiny station lost in the mountains, where Indians and horses were awaiting them.

As they started up a winding mountain path that bordered the chasm of a river bed it began to drizzle. It drizzled so hard and so fast that in a few minutes the women's finery, wasp waists, fluted lace, wide skirts, veils, and high, laced shoes, became dripping wet in a lamentable, yet comic, fashion. Then Don Alfonso ordered the Indians who were following them, staggering under the weight of the baggage:

"Take the ponchos and the straw hats for the women out of the big bag."

"Arí—sí, master, su mercé," replied the Indians, complying with a nervous eagerness.

The caravan, with the patrones now shielded from the rain in wide-brimmed men's hats, rainproof, dark, and lustrous continued climbing up the peak for more than an hour. When they came to a crossroad they could see dwarf vegetation of straw and frailejones reaching out to a somber horizon. Then Don Alfonso, in a voice trembling with cold, announced to the women who were following him:

"This is where the plateau begins. The rain . . . I hope it will soon pass . . . Don't you want a little drink?"

"No. Just let's go on," answered the mother of the family with a gesture of obvious ill humor which on long horseback trips originates in the aching buttocks.

"And you?"

"I'm quite well, papa."

"Well . . . quite well fucked," added a sarcastic voice deep within the rebellious soul of the father.

From that moment on the trip became slow, wearisome and unbearable. The páramo, with its ceaseless whipping of wind and water, with its loneliness that intimidates and oppresses, imposed silence on them. It was a silence with the breath of fog on the lips, on the nose, a silence which was lightly shredded by the hoofs of the animals, by the misshapen feet of the Indians: scarred heels, calloused soles, swollen toes.

Almost at the end of the slope, the caravan had to make an unexpected halt. The lead horse of the patrón grande, su mercé, sniffed the ground, nervously pricked up his ears, and backed away a few steps, refusing to obey the spurs that were raking his flanks.

"What? . . . What?" the women questioned in chorus.

"This idiot horse is scared stiff. I don't know . . . He saw something . . . He's cunning . . . José, Juan, Andrés, everyone!" the master shouted. He had to have an explanation from his peones.

"Little master . . . ," someone replied, and a group of Indians quickly materialized around the problem of Don Alfonso.

"He won't go on," the inexpert horseman said in an accusing voice while he punished the beast.

"Just wait a minute, little master," murmured the youngest and cleverest peón.

Pereira would have willingly responded negatively, striking out on that uncertain route, over the untrod wet grass, which was veiled by mist and tortured and groaning with a feverish pulsation of toads and small marsh animals. But the accursed horse, the women, his inexperience . . . only seldom had he visited his hacienda and then in the summer, with a bright sun, and the earth dry. The Indians, who after an inspection told him how dangerous it would be to go on without a guide to avoid the holes in the quagmire worsened by the recent storms, finally calmed him.

"O.K. Who goes first?"

"Andrés. He knows how. He knows the way, pa-troncitu."

"Then . . . let's go."

"Not like this. The animal will just put his hoof in and take it right out again. We gotta carry you."

"Ah! I see."

"Sí, little father."

"You, José, since you're the strongest you can take Señora Blanquita."

Señora Blanquita de Pereira, mother of the distin-guished family, was a sow who weighed at least one hundred and sixty pounds. Don Alfonso went on:

"Andrés, who'll have to go in the lead, will carry me and Juan will take Lolita. Let the rest carry the bag-gage."

After wiping their faces, wet with sweat and drizzle, on their shirtsleeves, after rolling up their denim pants to the thigh, and after taking out their ponchos and folding them corner to corner in Apache style, the Indians named by the master humbly presented their backs so the members of the Pereira family could dismount from the animals and mount them.

With all the care that such precious cargos de-served, the three peones advanced into the quagmire:

Squish . . . Squish . . . Squish . . .

Andrés, weighted down by Don Alfonso, went in front. It wasn't a steady march. It was an instinctive measuring of the danger with the feet. It was a slow sink-ing and rising in the mud. It was a harmonious note amid the orchestra of the toads and marsh animals:

Squiiish . . . Squiiish . . . Squiiish . . .

And yet at the same time it was the fear of a mis-step that imposed silence, that increased the misery of their condition, that was making the wind freeze, that made the fog thick, that added a complaining tone to the respiration of both man and beast:

Oooof . . . Oooof . . . Oooof . . .

The long and vexing boredom wrung a monologue of disjointed reflections from Don Alfonso: "They say that those who die in the cold páramo wear a grimace of laughter. The soroche. The altitude sickness . . . How right the gringos are in demanding I build a road. But me . . . Me chosen for such a thing . . . Patience . . . Patience? What crap! . . . This is a frozen version of Hell . . . *They* know . . . And the one who knows, knows . . . Why? They're people accustomed to a better life. They come to educate us. They bring us progress in huge doses, by the handfuls. To us . . . Ha . . . Ha . . . Ha . . . My father. Whiskers, frock coat, and umbrella in the city. Chaps, poncho, and straw hat in the country . . . My father, instead of just being cruel to his Indians and branding them on the forehead or chest with red hot irons, like cattle, should have organized them into large co-operative work groups . . . that would have spared me this fuckin' trip. Goddamit . . . But when the old man was alive the only one who had a practical mind was President García Moreno. *He* knew how to use the criminals and the Indians in the construction of the road to Riobamba. All to the tune of the lash . . . Ah! The lash that cured the soroche when crossing the páramos of Mount Chimborazo, that raised up the fallen ones, that tamed the rebels. The lash of progress. A flawless man, a great man." So deep was Don Alfonso's emotion when he evoked that historic figure that he gave a start of involuntary delight on the back of the Indian. Andrés, caught unaware by that movement of stupid violence, lost his balance and broke the fall of his precious cargo by sinking his hands into the muck clear up to his elbows.

"Goddamit! You clumsy fool!" the rider protested, seizing the Indian's greasy hair with both hands.

"Aaaay!!" shrieked the women.

But Don Alfonso didn't fall. Miraculously he kept his balance, clinging with his knees and digging his spurs into the body of the man who had tried to play him such a scurvy trick.

"Little master . . . ," mumbled Andrés in a tone beseeching pardon for his guilt while he straightened up dripping mud and fright.

After a brief dialogue, the small caravan continued its way. Because of the perils and the monotony of the march, Doña Blanca thought about Our Lady of Pompeya, of her faithful devotion to her. It was a real miracle to navigate that sea of mud. "A tangible miracle . . . an unbelievable miracle," the ingenuous señora thought more than once, and went on imagining the liturgical pomp of the fiesta with which her friends would honor the Virgin next month. But nevertheless she, Doña Blanca Chanique de Pereira, would be absent. Absent, too, would be her furs, her lace, her rings, her necklaces, her generosity, her body with its restless and amorous longings in spite of the years. In spite of the years . . . *That?* . . . She tried to appease *that* after the social affair, the public affair. Yes. When all the lights in the temple were extinguished, when discreet shadow lay along the corners of the naves and the organ silent in the choir loft; when it seemed that from the clusters and Eucharistic spicas— adornment and glory of the Solomonic columns of the altars—there streamed a vapor of incense, of faded roses, of cosmetics of beatas, of sweat of Indians; when her soul, her poor honorable wife's soul so seldom cared for by her husband, felt itself drawn by a desire to confide, by a devilish and yet mystical bashfulness, by impulses which obliged her to await, at the threshold to the sacristy, the tender counsel of Father Uzcátegei, her confessor. And so . . . And so at least . . .

"Are you well, my child?" asked Doña Blanca, trying to banish her memories.

"Sí. It's just getting used to it," answered the girl who liked the odor rising from the Indian to whom she was clinging in order not to fall, because it reminded her of her seducer. "Less stinking and hotter than his . . . when his hands advanced over the intimacies of my body. The wretch! If he had only loved me. The coward! To flee, to abandon me in such a situation. I was a fool. I . . . I'm the only one to blame. I was incapable of protesting against his caresses, his lies . . . I, too . . . ," the young girl told herself over and over, with an obsession so strong that it weatherproofed her, sheltering her from the cold, the wind, and the mist.

On the other hand, in the minds of the Indians— those who cared for the horses, those who carried the baggage, those who went ahead burdened by the weight of the patrones—there blossomed and faded only the anxieties of their immediate needs: that the roasted corn or barley flour supplies for the trip would last; that the mist would soon lift so they could see the last of the quagmire; that it wouldn't be long before they returned to their huts; that all was well on their huasipungos. They were worried about their children, their wives, their parents, their guinea pigs, their pigs, their crops. They worried that the masters who were returning would issue painful orders, impossible to fulfill, that the water, the earth, the ponchos, the work-shirts . . . Against the background of all these worries, only Andrés, as a responsible guide, was recalling the instructions of father Chiliquinga: "You mustn't step where the grass isn't firm, where the water is clear . . . You mustn't lift one foot until the other is firmly planted . . . Walk on tiptoe so that the toes can warn you . . . Just take it easy . . . easy . . ."

Twilight was falling as the cavalcade entered the village of Tomachi. Winter, with the bitter winds off the nearby páramo, the misery and idleness of the people, and the shadow of the giant intimidating peaks, had made that village a nest of muck, of garbage, of sadness, with a huddled-up defensive attitude. The huts huddled all along the single muddy street; the children huddled in the doorways of the huts playing with the putrid mud, their teeth chattering with chronic malarial fever; the women huddled over the open hearths, morning and night, to boil their barley mash or their potato soup; the men, from six in the morning till six at night, huddled over their work in the fields, in the mountains, in the páramo, or vanished along the trails behind their mules that carry produce to the neighboring villages; huddled, too, was the murmur of the water in the ditch tattooed along the street—the ditch of dirty water where the animals from the nearby huasipungos drank, where pigs made beds of mud to renew their passions, where children crouched on all fours to drink, where drunkards urinated.

At that hour, through the gorge that looked toward the valley, there rushed an icy wind, a rainy season afternoon wind, a wind that swept the plumes of smoke from the huts that could now be seen scattered along the slopes.

The travelers gazed with a hopeful smile at the first house in the village—a small building, with a thatched roof, with the porch open to the street, with unplastered adobe walls, with blackened doors orphaned of windows.

"It's closed," remarked the master in a reproachful voice, as though someone should have been there expecting him.

"That's because Don Braulio is a mule driver,

patroncitu," explained one of the Indians.

"Mule driver," repeated Don Alfonso while he was thinking: "Why doesn't this man have to account to me? Why? Everyone in this village is tied somehow to the hacienda. To my hacienda, goddamit. That's what my father used to say."

On the porch of that hovel, which seemed to be long abandoned, such was the silence, such the age, such the solitude, there were only two black pigs, who were rooting in the not-very-wet-dirt floor, doubtless to enlarge the hollow of their bed. Further, on the street itself, a few skeletal dogs, their rib cage like a half-opened accordion, were fighting over a carrion bone that must have rolled through the entire village.

Near the plaza, an odor of tender eucalyptus wood and of dried cow dung, like the breath of a sick and defenseless animal, came from the sordid dwellings which were distributed in two rows, like a putrid, scanty, and uneven set of teeth—like those of an old witch—and enveloped the travelers, offering them a weird assurance of protection. From the porch of one of those small huts, where there hung the skinned and eviscerated carcass of a lamb, a man came out, a peasant with a poncho, hemp sandals, and a childlike curiosity in his glance. The peasant murmured in the peculiar tone of the farmer:

"Good afternoon, patrones."

"Good afternoon. Who are you? What's your name?" asked Don Alfonso in return.

"Calupiña, pes."

"Ah! Sí. And how are you?"

"Still kicking! And you—su merced?"

"Can't complain."

The caravan of masters and Indians passed by without giving any more thought to the words of the cholo who, after throwing the lamb viscera which he had held in his hands into a basket, stood agape, watching the imposing figures of the Pereira family as they faded into the distance. Also, the half-breed woman who lived next door, an old, skinny, and greasy woman whom they called Miche, "mother cat of the babies," because of her numerous litters by unknown fathers, spied with almost infantile curiosity and fear on the family from Cuchitambo, while entrenched behind an enormous pan loaded with fried pork and corn. Further down, in front of a hut of ample size and not so sad as the others, two girls—marriageable cholas, with hemp sandals and skirts—were shouting in the middle of the street in the unfeminine way appropriate to their age. They were the daughters of old Melchor Espíndola. The younger, chubbier, and darker was shaking off something that clung like a topknot to her head.

"*Ay . . . Ay . . . Ay . . .* !"

"Just wait! Waiiit . . . !" shrieked the other, trying to control her sister, as if she were a stubborn child, until with a violence, half angry and half playful, she succeeded in knocking to the ground the inopportune addition to the hair of the noisier girl. A black spider, very black, with thick velvety legs vanished quickly through a hole in a fence of cactus plants.

The fright of the impudent girls quickly evaporated in the surprise of seeing people from the capital: the odor, the clothes, the adornments, the cosmetics.

"Good afternoon," said one.

"Good afternoon, ladies," the other ratified.

"Good afternoon, children," answered Doña Blanca with the expression of a victim, while Don Alfonso looked at the girls with the sly smile of a satyr in ambush.

Before a store with stone steps at the threshold and in shade deep enough to hide its wretchedness and the poor quality of merchandise it exhibited, there stood a drove of mules. This was the store of taita Timoteo Peña, where he sold brandy (well-watered, so it did no harm), bread, homemade tallow candles, corn flour, barley flour, wheat flour, salt, pan sugar, and a few medicines, and where the mule drivers could come to take their drinks and leave behind the news they had picked up along the roads.

In the doorway of the telegraph office, the operator, a small, nervous, and slightly effeminate cholo, was playing a turn-of-the-century dance tune, a pasillo, on his guitar.

Toward the end of the street, in an enormous and abandoned plaza, the church balanced the antiquity of its thick walls on long supports, like a venerable cripple who was able to escape from the hospital of time by going on crutches. The ancient, wrinkled quality of the façade contrasted with the gold of the high altar and with the jewels, ornaments, and dress of the Virgin of the Spoon. She was the patroness of the village, at whose feet Indians and peasants, intimidated by ancestral fears and by the harsh experiences of reality, had daily divested themselves of their savings, so that the most Holy and Miraculous Lady could buy herself, and shine in, her heavenly formal finery.

From the priest's home, the only house with a tile roof, and exhibiting part of the jewels that the Virgin of the Spoon had been kind enough to lend her, the priest's concubine, alias "his niece," the baggage with pompous breasts and hips, distrustful glance, and gross features, whom the holy father had brought with him from the capital, stepped out just at that moment with a container of garbage. She dumped the trash in the open drain in the street and stood transfixed, staring at the Pereira family's cavalcade.

THE HOPE for a well-earned rest evoked a rare happiness in the travelers when they glimpsed the hacienda manor with its corrals and sheds, a white spot on the dark green slope. The manor stood like a fortress amid a scattered army of drab huts.

When the mayordomo saw the patrones he stopped his mule dead. The mule was an indispensable complement of his face, his personality, his abundant sex-drive, his foul smells of cow dung and rotting leather. He forced her to sit down on her haunches in a show of typical cholo efficiency and braggadocio. And in his rapid-fire delivery, his breath foul with the rotten-pear odor of a hangover from raw brandy and from sour corn liquor, he greeted them:

"May God give us a good afternoon, patroncitos."

He quickly took off his hat, revealing a head of greasy hair falling in sticky, sweaty locks over his forehead.

"Good afternoon, Policarpio."

"I'm sick to death of such a rain. The whole damn day. What's up, pes? The little miss came along too?"

Without answering the cholo's inopportune question Don Alfonso immediately asked about the behavior of the Indians, about the chances of acquiring the timber-lands, about the crops, about the mingas . . .

"I have great plans. The future of my children demands it," the master concluded.

"Ooooh . . . He's changed. When did he ever care about anything? Now they'll really notice what's going on . . . The Indians, the crops, the timber. What for, pes? And his children . . . He says his children . . . He has just one. The niña Lolita. What children did he mean? Perhaps the big one is pregnant. Síííí . . . She seems a little fat . . . ," the cholo Policarpio thought, doubting the sanity of his patrón. Never before had he asked those questions; never before had he shown so much interest in the affairs of the hacienda.

The old Cuchitambo manor house greeted the travelers with its stone-paved patio; its smell of rotting grass and dried cow dung; the epileptic manifestations of the dogs, the mumbling murmur of the Quechua chatter of the Indian servant girls; the lowing of the cows and calves; the ample verandah with its rustic pillars adorned with dried-up stuffed deer-heads as a kind of capital, which served as racks for saddles, bridles, lassos, ropes, rags; the sheepfold stuck on to the butt of the building and separated from it by a fence of worm-eaten sticks and rusty wire, which was an enclosure for sheep and calves; and, above all, it greeted them with that perfume of old memories—some of enjoyment, others of cruelty, but the majority of absolute power over the local Indians.

After everything was in order in the house of the patrones, the Indians who had served as guides and beasts of burden for the caravan scattered over the area, using the most difficult short cuts, the most tortuous paths. They headed for their huasipungos.

Andrés Chiliquinga, instead of following the route

that could take him to his parents' hut—his taita had died of colic a few years before, his mother now lived with three younger children and a (male) friend who appeared and disappeared by turns—plunged into the woods. For roughly two years now the Indian Chiliquinga had been making this same trip. With his mistrust, his suspicions, his furtive glances, within the most hidden and dark recesses of the great chaparral he had made for himself a secret passageway to the hut where he was awaited by Cunshi's love and by his baby, and where he could eat his thick corn soup in peace. Yes. He had been doing that for two years. He had mocked the vigilance of the mayordomo, had disobeyed the abusive threats of the local priest in order to live with the Indian girl who had bewitched him, who smelled so nice to him, who, when he came near her, heated the blood in his veins with such sweet spirit that, when he talked to her, everything took on a different hue—the work became less cruel, nature less hard, and life itself less unjust. They, the mayordomo and the cura, had tried to get him to marry a young Indian from the Filocorrales hacienda and so increase the number of the master's farmhands. Ah! But he had tricked them and had gone to live with his Cunshi in a hut he had built on the edge of the large ravine. Later . . . everyone had to pretend to overlook it. But the master . . . the master who had arrived so unexpectedly. What would he say? Whaaat? The fear and the mistrust he had felt in his first days with Cunshi returned to torture him. The words of the holy priest echoed in his mind: "Savages. They refuse to follow the way of God. Of our Beloved Father, the brutes. They shall roast in Hell." In those moments he pictured Hell as an enormous settlement of Indians. There were no whites there, no priests, no mayordomos, nor sheriffs. In spite of its flames, its monstrous beasts, the absence of such personages soothed him greatly. And on arriving at the hut, his soul burdened with worry, Andrés Chiliquinga called:

"Cunshiiii!"

She was not there, in the shadow of the hovel. His shout, half anxious, half angry, woke up the baby who had been asleep in a corner wrapped in dirty coarse woolens.

"Cunshiiii!"

From the chaparral thickets, very near the huasipungo, where the Indian girl, making use of the dying light, was gathering dry branches for the fire, there rose a weak, frightened voice:

"Hmm??"

"Where are you, pes?"

"Pickin' up firewood."

"Pickin' up firewood? Crap! And here's the baby yelling his head off," cried the Indian in a threatening tone. He didn't know whether to show tenderness or anger. His woman, a refuge in his memory, the warmth of pleasure of the mattress, was there; nothing had happened to her; she hadn't betrayed him; she hadn't been violated. And in spite of the truth of her excuse, in spite of its obviousness, the morbid urges that he felt inside— a desire to sate his passion with bites and blows—made him cry out:

"You liar!"

"Li . . ."

With a catlike bound he seized the girl by the hair. She dropped the firewood that she had gathered and cowered under some century plants like a hen awaiting the cock. If someone had tried to protect her she would have turned on him immediately to warn him furiously: "You busybody. Let him hit me, kill me, cut me to pieces, that's why he's my husband, that's why he's my own man."

After shaking her and beating her, Andrés Chiliquinga, with the labored breathing of a madman, dragged
his victim inside the hut. And there, stretched out on the
bare dirt floor—she, soft and trembling from his recent
blows, her body complaining and gently writhing with
tender resentment, and he, crazed with anger and passion, his muscles ready, gasping with guilty desire—they
came together, creating in their fleeting pleasure contours
of voluptuousness, which bordered on the twitching edges
of vengeance, of despair, of agony.

"Ay . . . Ay . . . Ay . . ."

"My darling."

Knotted in a savage tenderness, they rolled very
close to the hearth. And feeling themselves, as usual in
such moments while sheltering each other, far—stupefying forgetfulness—from all the injustice, from all the
humiliation and sacrifice which existed outside the hut,
they fell asleep, covered by the warmth of their own
bodies, by the poncho still soaked from the páramo, by
the fury of the lice.

THE DRIZZLE of the prolonged winter increased the Pereira family's boredom. On clear mornings Don Alfonso would mount his black mule—he preferred her because of her gentleness and meekness—and set out along the path through the chaparral on the other bank of the river. When he reached the village he usually stopped for a short time at the sheriff's store. The sheriff was a cholo of wrinkled robustness who never removed his poncho, his unshined calfskin shoes, or his dilapidated hat; nor did he ever lose his pride in having built his home by honestly saving up the fines, the taxes, and the fiscal contributions which found their way to the sheriff's office. Yes, it had become customary for Don Alfonso to have a glass of brandy with a dash of lemon and to listen to the chatter, sometimes ingenuous, sometimes cynical, of this authority when he came into Tomachi.

"There's no one. No one like me . . . me, Jacinto Quintana . . . and like One-Eyed Rodríguez, goddamit . . . to know the Indians' laziness and brazenness and how to cure these ailments by the whip, the club and the bullet."

"Well. You're probably right."

"Pes, I have been a foreman a few times."

"Really?"

This cholo, so successful as sheriff, bartender, and foreman, could also be recommended as a good Christian: he heard the entire mass of Sundays, he believed in the sermons of the priest and in miracles of the saints, and, like a model husband, had two children by his chola Juana; he had no concubine among the local half-breed women; he slaked his sexual thirst on the Indian women whom he succeeded in violating in the ditches. Like a big slob, he changed his underwear every month, and his feet stank of rotting leather.

"Here, have some of this. This is the real stuff brought in from up-country. Juana prepares it with fig leaves."

"And what's wrong with Juana? I don't see her."

"Pes, she's in the kitchen. Juanaaa! The patrón is here from Cuchitambo."

"I'm comi-i-i-ing."

Almost always the woman—appetizing humbleness in her eyes, bronze skin, generous hips, her black hair in two braids tied with candlewicks, her shapely arms bare to the elbow—would appear through a soot-covered door that opened onto the porch facing the road, where there was a stone slab laden with trays of cinnamon candy, boiled beef entrails, and avocados to sell to the Indians. At sight of the omnipotent gentleman the chola blushed, slid her hands down along her hips, and murmured:

"Pes, how is the missus?"

"All right."

"And your little girl?"

"So-so."

"Oooh?"

"You're looking plumper, and better."

"You're looking at me with kindly eyes."

Then Juana repaid the gallantry of the landowner by ordering her husband to serve their visitor another glass of brandy.

"Another?" protested Don Alfonso in a voice that seemed to disguise a request.

"What's wrong, pes? Is it going to hurt you?"

"Hurt me, no . . . But . . ."

"He . . . Hee . . . Hee . . ."

While the husband would go for the brandy, Pereira would reward Juana with one or two amorous pinches on the breast or on the buttocks. Almost always at those moments the chola's youngest son would be present—he was a year and a few months old—crawling on the floor and exhibiting his innocent sexual organ.

"May he grow up healthy," the landlord commented, trying to excuse his urban repugnance when the infant, snotty and dirty, drew near him.

"He's a regular glutton," the woman commented.

"Yes, but . . ."

"Come, come, my little guagua."

Don Alfonso's excursions usually wound up at the priest's home. The landowner and the priest would often engage in long, weighty and, occasionally, amusing conversations: about the country, progress, democracy, morals, or politics. Don Alfonso, using and abusing his liberal opinions, gave the priest his complete confidence and deep friendship. The parish priest in his turn offered Christian gratitude and understanding, and allied himself with the master of the valley and mountain with all his material and spiritual powers.

"If all the priests were like this one the world would be a paradise," affirmed the one.

"His generosity and his energy make him a good man. God has touched his heart in secret," the other would proclaim.

The priest's first favor was to help Pereira buy the

section of land owned by the Ruata brothers, two peasant
orphans who were old enough to marry and who sub-
limated their bachelorhood by composing sonnets to the
Virgin. And therefore they were at the mercy of the
cleric's advice and opinions. Their land was in the chaparral at the entrance to the all-but-savage forest. Other
favors followed.

When someone dared to reproach Don Alfonso for
his friendship with the priest, the worthy landowner
would throw back his shoulders and, assuming the attitude of a famous hero, exclaim:

"You can't see any further than your noses. I have
my plans. He is a very important part of them."

And, in truth, Pereira was not very far wrong. One
afternoon, in the shade of the vines that wove a loose
curtain between the pillars of the priest's entry-way, the
cleric and the landowner were discussing the Guamaní
affair and the Indians.

"That old Isidro must be a thief. You can tell by
his face," said the landowner.

"Rather he's a man who knows the value of land, the
value of the forests and of the Indians," countered the
priest.

"But that hasn't got him anything. Not at all."

"Who knows?"

"Woods. Marshlands . . ."

"And Indians, my dear friend."

"Indians!"

"Besides. If you don't want to buy . . ."

The priest threw his head back against the chair on
which he rested, in order to sink into a slightly theat-
rical pause. He had to make sure of his commission in the
affair. The money was almost in his hands. Even God
said, "God helps those who help themselves." Ah! As
long as he didn't help himself to the cactus and the
varmints of the chaparral thickets, he'd be fine.

"Well . . . want to . . . as for wanting to . . . ," muttered Don Alfonso softly, trying to break the priest's silence while the priest, in a sweetly mocking tone, insisted:

"With the Indians, too?"

"Of course. You understand that the lands without the Indians are worth nothing."

"And what Indians! All yours, all serfs, very meek. You can do what you like with those people."

"I have heard that nearly all of them are single. An unmarried Indian is only worth half. Without children, without wife or family."

"And so what?"

"It seems you don't understand. Who'll take care of the herding, the household chores, the felling of timber? Who'll take part in the mingas?"

"I see. There are more than five hundred. More than five hundred who, thanks to my patience, my faith, my counsel, and my threats, I have made follow the way of the Lord. Now they are ready for . . ." He was going to say, "for sale," but the word seemed too harsh, and, so after a slight hesitation, he continued, "For work. You'll see. The young Indians will cost you very little; they'll be almost a gift."

"Yes. It seems . . ."

"The only thing they require to be content is their huasipungos."

"But that itself can be annoying."

"But they have to live somewhere!"

"The huasipungos, the produce we give them, the brandy, the credit we allow them."

"Fairy tales! You'll see, you'll see, Don Alfonsito."

He quickly changed the subject to the purchase of the Guamaní lands.

"Since I have no axe to grind and can't take sides,

I'll try to serve as a link between you two landowners. I feel confident. The Divine Being will guide our steps."

"I hope so."

"That's how it will be."

And finally, when offers and commissions had been agreed on, when everything had been settled in a cynical and unscrupulous informality, the priest declared:

"Let's put aside for a moment any stingy thoughts, any . . . Hee . . . Hee . . . Hee . . . It seems unbelievable . . . The purchase will assure you a brilliant future. It's not just the lands and the Indians that we've been discussing. No . . . On the mountain slopes there are still some Indians as uncivilized as the cattle on the páramo. Indians not registered in the owner's books, whom, with Christian prudence and charity, we can be putting in our corral. Do you follow me? Me . . . I'll take charge of that. What else could you want?"

"Ah! Thank you. But isn't all this a dream?"

"I'm familiar with these affairs. I know. That's why I'm telling you. And since you are a big entrepreneur . . . The two of us can . . ."

"Of course."

THE PEREIRA GIRL bore her child without any further complications. Two Indian midwives and Doña Blanca secretly assisted at the birth. The new-born infant's problem began when the mother's milk dried up. Don Alfonso, who in these times was lord and master of Guamaní and its Indians, solved the problem by shouting:

"Get a few Indian mothers who are nursing their babies. But robust, healthy. We'll have to choose well."

The mayordomo obeyed the order with an air of mystery, but competently. And that very afternoon, herding a group of Indian women, he came to the great hall of the manor house. This hall faced the patio. The patrones, husband and wife, looked once and then again at each one of the young women. But it was Doña Blanca who, with the repugnance of an irrepressible ill humor that puckered her lips, had the job of poking and handling the breasts and the infants of the candidates to nurse her grandson.

"Lift up your shawl."

"Little mistress . . ."

"I won't do anything. I'm just looking."

"Pretty mistress . . ."

The Indian girl spoken to, with the fear and humility

of one who has suffered treacherous abuses, raised a corner of the coarse woolen cloth that covered her baby. Swaddled in filthy rags like an Egyptian mummy, a tender infant with swollen eyelids, pallid, sad, black-haired, and emitting a nauseating odor, moved his head.

"Do you have plenty of milk?"

"Sí mistress, su mercé."

"It doesn't seem like it. The baby is quite puny."

"We have to be very careful," put in Pereira.

"We'll see yours now," continued Doña Blanca addressing another one of the Indian women waiting there.

After a tedious examination of the mothers and their infants, with a steady stream of pessimistic comments from the mayordomo and from the patrón, they selected a woman who seemed robust and clean.

"What do you think of her?" asked the wife, looking at Pereira.

"Yes, O.K. That's better. But have her bathe in the river. If there's time. It's not too late. Oh! And let her leave the child in her hut."

"She can't do that, patrón," put in the mayordomo.

"Why not?"

"She lives all alone, pes."

"That's easily fixed. You take care of the boy until she's free."

"Me? Ave María. And who, pes . . . ?"

"Don't you have an Indian girl working in your house?"

"Yes, that's right. What will people say? Hee . . . Hee . . . Hee . . . Policarpio just came in with a little baby . . . Just like a woman . . ."

The wet nurse, well scrubbed—to the patrón's liking—and with a great silent and secret ache caused by her worry for her son's fate, took her place at the foot of the cradle of the Pereira grandchild. Unfortunately she didn't last long. In a few weeks the mayordomo brought the news of her little son's death.

"The servant girl didn't know how. Really stupid . . . It's not my fault. What could I have done for him? He was scrawny . . . Wrinkled like a prune."

". . . Gasping for air all day long . . . Had diarrhea, too . . . He was in sad shape . . ."

The Indian mother, on hearing about her son, couldn't say a single word; every part of her body had become rigid, throttled, and useless, but she bowed her head and leaned on the kitchen wall. Then, like an automaton, she did her chores the rest of the afternoon, and that night she fled the house, the valley, and the village. No one ever learned where she went or what she did.

Without losing a minute, the landowner again commanded the mayordomo:

"You'll have to bring in some more Indians."

"Sí, patrón."

"The best ones."

"We'll do that."

The cholo Policarpio looked for and found the women he needed working the potato patch. When they noticed the man's presence—he who was so conniving, cruel, and haughty with them—they dug their farm implements among the weeds in the furrows with a feigned zeal and looked at him surreptitiously.

"Hey!" shouted the cholo from the fence.

No one took the trouble to answer. It was better he should believe that . . .

"Where did you leave your babies? I want to see them!" insisted the mayordomo.

Faced with such a strange request, unusual and absurd, the women straightened up and, open-mouthed, stared at the man who cried:

"Don't you hear me?"

"No."

"I said where did you leave the guaguas?"

The Indian women turned their heads towards some thickets in the ditch where the potato patch ended.

"O.K. Just leave this for a while. Let's take a look at the guaguas, pes," the cholo said, directing his mule toward the place that the Indian women had indicated with their eyes.

As the group of women drew near the shade of the chaparral, a noise, as of complaint, was growing stronger; it was a fluttering of flight among the fallen leaves, a mystery of infantile monologue that questions and engenders friendship and trust in all things, a tired plaint of frustrated longing—a noise that became clear and distressing.

It was the little ones left by the Indian women at the edge of their work area—for three, four, sometimes five hours. The older children, charged with the care of the younger ones, when they grew aware of the unexpected visit, hurried—without rhyme or reason, with a guilty feeling—to fulfil their duties. "When the guagua cries just give him some porridge . . . Watch out so he doesn't roll into the hole . . . If he eats dirt or puts caca in his mouth take it away from him . . ." And it was always like this. Only at the last minute and when aware of the possible punishment did the big ones, who were three or four years old, comply hastily with the order of their parents by stuffing the desperate, hungry mouths of the little ones with a rough wooden spoon containing the cold and decomposed food ladled from an earthen jar covered with cabbage leaves.

From the restless infantile troop scattered on the ground, larvae who tried to rise from the earth with a distrustful grumbling, there arose a demanding murmur on sight of their mothers who reproached them each in her own way:

"Bad children."

"Ave María."

"Just like goats, like devils."

"Taiticu will just kill you."

"I'll have to tie you with a lasso."

"Outlaws."

"Mama! Mama! Ooh . . . ooh . . . !"

"What are you saying, goddamit?" asked the mayordomo, always jealous of his authority before the Indians.

"Pes, nothing, su mercé."

"They're hungry."

"They're cold."

"They just want to be annoying."

"Show me the youngest," said the cholo, trying to imitate the patrón.

The man's command, like the thunder of Taita Dios to the children's fright, caused a fearful silence among them, and everything, absolutely everything, became clear in the scene that extended from the shade of the chaparral to the unevenness of the terrain that formed the gully. The distressful mummification of the first vital needs in a prison of coarse woolen swathing—an arabesque of vivid colors woven in the huasipungo. Sí. The mummification necessary to stifle the tummy aches caused by the stale porridge and the cold potatoes, necessary to hold and hide the chafed skin of legs and buttocks, the reddened stench of a twenty-four hours' accumulation of urine and excrement. The wit and caprice of the bigger ones also rose to the heights of delight. They had invented an exotic toyshop of mud and clay objects, abstract and yet real, modeled in the subconscious truth of their hands, objects which they fought over, tooth and nail, among tears and threats. In a synthesis of pain and

abandonment, an Indian boy, about five years old, huddled beneath a poncho, as if hatching a surprise that
burned like a hot iron. After making a series of tragic
grimaces he raised himself to a crouch and, with his pants
still dripping, turned his head to look, in a fatigue of
agony, at a bloody stain he had left on the ground. Then
he took a few steps and threw himself face down on the
grass. He tried to stifle the violent pain gnawing at his
vitals and nerves.

The mayordomo, inspired by the example and the
teaching of the patrones, carefully inspected the children.

"Not a single healthy one. Every single one looks
peculiar. The patrona Doña Blanquita won't want any
such garbage."

With a half ingenuous and half idiotic smile, the
children concerned—those who were old enough to understand—tried to listen to the mayordomo's opinion, but all
their expressions of joy or mockery were diluted by the
shiver of malarial fever, the languor of chronic anemia,
the itch of an incurable mange, or by the grimace of a
stomach pang.

The cholo, without knowing what to do, persisted in
his lamentations:

"Why, pes, don't you suckle the guaguas? Maybe
your milk isn't good for them, you Indian whores?"

"Ha, ha, ha! Indian whores the patrún mayordomo
called us," murmured the chorus of women. And one, the
oldest, said:

"The guaguas are really tricky, pes."

"Tricky, hell."

"Do you think they eat the things that a poor woman
leaves them? Porridge, too . . . roast corn, too . . ."

"Everything's the same to them."

"Goddamit! And what do I take to the mistress,
pes? Her baby is crying his head off for milk. There's

good food, good dark beer, and good treatment for the wetnurses. Better than for the housemaids, for the cooks, for the permanent household help, better than for the caretakers, Oooh . . . a real pleasure, pes. But always providing that she is robust, with tits as healthy as a Jersey cow."

The mayordomo's remarks, and the word that had spread about the surfeit and good treatment that they had given the first longa who serviced the baby, aroused the greed of the mothers. Each one hurriedly ran for her off-spring and immediately exhibited him with a marketing type of deceit and noise before the eyes of the cholo Policarpio.

"Look, patroncitu."

"Just look, pes."

"Look at mine."

"Mine, too."

"Mine certainly isn't thin at all," shouted one Indian, her hoarse voice dominating the general hubbub. Without any scruples, she violently lifted her son on high, like a gift, a thing of joy, a flag of rags and stenches. Her example caught on. The majority immediately imitated the hoarse-voiced woman. Others, on the other hand, un-blushingly took out their breasts and squeezed them to weave threads of milk in the impassive face of the mule which the mayordomo was riding.

"Don't squirt your milk in the animal's eyes, god-damit!"

"Patroncituuu."

"Taiticuuu."

"Bonituuu."

"Look, pes."

"If the worst comes to the worst, the poor mule will die of nerves, like a human," observed the cholo, making his beast rear with his spurs, in order to save her from the desperate women.

"What are we, *pes*, devils?"

"What are we, *pes*, witches?"

"It's like milk from the Almighty Father—Taita Diosito."

"Wait! Hold on!" shouted Policarpio.

"Take me!"

"Me, too!"

"Oooh . . . !"

"Look at my guagua!"

"Look at my breasts!"

"Look here, pes!"

"Look at me, hard!"

The soliciting voices of the women, mixed with the plaints of the children and the protest of the mayordomo filled the countryside with a tumult like that in a marketplace.

"I know the one I want, goddamit. Wait, I said! You stupid Indians! You, Juana Quishpe. You, Rosario Caguango. You, Catota . . . Let's go . . . The mistress herself will say what seems fair to her," the rider ordered, and then made the women he had selected go before him.

Still stunned by their rotten luck, the chorus of rejected longas asked in a bitter plaintive tone:

"And what about us, ga?"

"Back to work, goddamit."

"Oooh . . ."

"If you don't finish the patch on that side, you'll get what's coming to you. You Indian bitches!"

"Indian bitches . . . Indian whores . . . That's all the taita mayordomo knows," growled the women in low mocking tones as they lazily returned to their backbreaking work on the crop, while in the shade of the chaparral and on the slope of the deep gully the crying, anxieties, hunger, and fanciful mumbling of the little ones swelled in volume.

At noon the troop of longas took a respite from

the oppressiveness of their work, a twelve-o'clock break to eat the roast corn and barley flour and to stretch out on the ground, staring stupidly with animal indifference at the distant landscape where a mustard-plaster sun was beating down. Happy moments for the voracity of the young ones: the tit, the cold food, the maternal presence—grumbling, omnipotent, full of reproaches and threats, but warm, tender, and good.

THE PURCHASE of Guamaní and the many expenses, some necessary and others not, of the last few months on the hacienda exhausted the money that his uncle had turned over to Don Alfonso Pereira. The latter, day by day, was becoming more nervous and demanding with the mayordomo, with the huasicamas, and with the Indians. When he learned that firewood and charcoal were much in demand among the haulers who sold them in the neighboring villages, he ordered the beginning of the exploitation of the woods on the mountain several kilometers away from the manor house.

"It's going to take twenty Indians, patrón," Policarpio informed him.

"Twenty or forty. As many as you need."

"And a foreman also, pes."

"A foreman?"

"Gabriel Rodríguez is good in such matters. Felling of trees, firewood, cutting, charcoal ovens."

"Well, then? Let's get going."

"Right away, su mercé."

The cholo Rodríguez, known as One-Eyed Rodríguez, was designated for the work. He was a pock-marked villager with coarse, dark features, a defiant glance in his good eye that would open and fix itself, distilling stupefying and challenging cynicism when answering or questioning the lower classes. On the other hand, Policarpio, according to his taste and caprice, selected the Indians from the huasipungos for the little job.

"See here . . . Andrés Chiliquinga! Tomorrow at dawn you'll have to go up on the mountain at Rinconada."

"At Rinconada?" repeated the Indian, interrupting his digging of a ditch at the edge of the field.

"Where we used to cut the firewood, pes. Others will be going along, too."

"Uh-huh."

"Now you know. Don't pull anything stupid later."

"Sí, arí, patrún," muttered Chiliquinga and stood motionless, without a sign that revealed his bitter disagreement, looking towards a spot lost on the nearest hill.

The mayordomo, who through long experience knew the meaning of that silence, insisted:

"Do you understand, you bastard?"

"Arí . . ."

"If you don't obey, you'll be screwed. The patrón will kick you out of your huasipungo."

Confronted with such a threat and twisting the always unexpressed fury of his hands into the handle of the hoe where he had left it leaning, the Indian tried to object:

"And what about Cunshi, patrún? The work will be long, pes."

"You'll be able to come back to stay on Sundays."

"And Cunshi?"

"You sniveling Indian! What has the woman to do with this?"

"Cunsh . . ."

"Cunshi will have to stay behind for the milking. She can't go that far away. That whole area is unhealthful. The poor longa would die of chills and fever."

"God keep . . ."

"You're trying to play stupid, you conniving Indian. Everyone has, pes, women, everyone has, pes, guaguas, and nobody starts to snivel . . . when the order's from the patrón. What is it, goddamit?"

"Please, su mercé . . ."

"Don't ask for any favors."

"It's so far."

"And so what?"

"It'd be better to make me a night watchman in the fields—a chacracama."

"You lazy Indian lout. So you'd be able to spend the whole day sleeping . . ."

"But, my good mayordomo, boniticu . . ."

"No more, carajo!"

Without listening to any more arguments, the cholo went away, leaving the Indian steeped in a bitter despair of impotence. How many months? How long would he have to stay buried up there in the chaparrals of the mountain? He didn't know. He couldn't know. There was no time limit, no future. Oh! To battle the drizzle, the marsh, the cold, the malaria, the early evening fatigue, O.K. And the prolonged separation from his longa and his guagua? That was impossible! What should he do? The mayordomo had told him irrevocably: "If you don't obey you'll be screwed. The patrón will kick you out of your huasipungo." That, that threat was the worst for him. None of his friends or family would have been capable of uprooting himself from the land. In a moment of hope, of clarity, of consolation, he thought: "Cunshi, taking the guagua, could accompany me to the mountain." But once more the cholo's words hammered in his heart, burying everything in a black, bottomless pit: "She's gotta stay behind . . . She's gotta stay behind for the milking." He couldn't think any more, not any more. Emotions, voices, and desires were knotted in his breast. The remainder of the day he worked furiously, with a fury that gnawed and scratched as he mercilessly dug with shovel and spade. And when he arrived at his hut, he didn't say a word. It was at dawn, when he filled his pouch with provisions, taking all the barley flour and all the roast corn, that she asked:

"Ave María, taiticu . . . Is the work really so far away?"

"Arí, sí."

"Why didn't you let your woman know before, pes?"

"Because I didn't feel like it, goddamit," shrieked the Indian, venting the anger which he had repressed since the evening before. It was always like this: a morbid impulse towards vengeance made him hurt his own friends, even the ones he cared for most.

"Can't we go with you, pes?"

"Go with me, go with me . . . You stick to me like a badly trained dog."

"That's just how it is, pes," insisted the woman, approaching him, desiring to emphasize her decision.

"No, goddamit! And what about the milking?" exclaimed Chiliquinga with reproach and in a threatening tone which admitted no argument. Then he thrust her away violently, as though to obliterate her with the violence of one who doesn't wish to see what he is doing, and strode out of the hut.

About this same time Doña Blanca, distraught with her proxy maternity, again complained:

"This stupid Indian's milk is killing my little son. It's good for nothing."

"It's no good," repeated Don Alfonso.

And even the little patrona, recovered, stupid, and as innocent as if she hadn't ever had a child, murmured:

"It's no good."

With the exhausted gesture of a hound who has investigated all the burrows without finding the tasty prey for the little one the mayordomo said:

"It'll be hard to find another longa."

But Don Alfonso, convinced, from his uncle's advice and his experience of these months in the country, that all difficulties could be resolved by sacrificing the Indians, shouted with the voice and gesture of an angry God:

"Goddamit! Why is it hard?"

"There aren't any, pes. The babies are so skinny. The women are so skinny."

"Bring them even if it kills them."

"We'll do it, patrón."

"And soon!"

"Now I remember. Cunshi who has shacked up with Chiliquinga has a guagua," announced the cholo Policarpio, his eyes brightening with the timely thought.

"Have her come."

"She is Chiliquinga's woman, pes. One of the Indians who went to work on the mountain. And because the Indian went unwillingly they say that every single night he comes back to sleep at least a little while with his sturdy woman."

"He comes back?"

"It's easy for them. By the short cuts, by the zigzag mountain paths. But when I catch that Indian he'll really get it."

"That's O.K. But the woman must come."

"We'll see to it, su mercé."

DUSK FELL EARLY on the gray silence of the wild chaparral at Rinconada. And the smell of the drizzle which tirelessly molded the mud and the muck of the footpaths, exasperatingly punctual every afternoon, along with the breath of the nearby marsh and the perfume of the moss, a greenish and rotting presence that covered the old trunks, saturated the atmosphere with a humidity that clung to the body and soul with the tenacity of a leech.

In the thick shade of evening—it was impossible to judge the hour—streaming water and mud, the Indians selected by the mayordomo of Cuchitambo for the work on the firewood and the charcoal straggled up to the only possible refuge in that place—a rickety architecture of moth-eaten poles, decaying mud wall sections, and filthy straw along the highest wall of the lower slope of the mountain. And some in silence, others muttering low about their bad luck or good luck in the day's tasks, huddled in the corners of the shed, allowing themselves to be lulled to sleep quickly by the musical monologue of the dripping water, by the skimpy orchestra of the toads and the crickets, by the noise of the wind and the rain on the foliage. And the night then became blacker, the anxiety of impotence became greater, and the feverish memories more vivid in the silence. But the drowsiness of weariness, bringing on a brutish sleep, surprised and conquered all the peons with a magical swiftness. They were bundles covered by ponchos, on which the lice, fleas, and even the ticks could glut themselves with Indian blood. Time moved to the rhythm of a pulse quickened by snores.

Stretched out next to one of the worm-eaten walls of the hut, alert to every little sign that could prevent his plan to flee, Andrés Chiliquinga hugged to his belly the sweaty fear that someone or something . . . *Sí*. He clenched in his work-worn hands the desire to crawl, to shout, to . . . No one responded or stirred at his first bold move. He crept like a cat, treading noiselessly over the pulverized straw cover on the floor. He stopped, listened, breathed deeply. He didn't measure the time nor the risk he would have to take by using the zigzag mountain path that cut across the hill—two, two and one-half hours at full speed; he thought only of the possibility of staying a short while with his Cunshi, his guagua, the chance of smelling the straw mattress in his hut, of patting his dog, of . . . "Take it easy, easy, you stupid Indian," he told himself as he passed by the bench against the door, the only slightly raised area in the place, where the foreman was sleeping. And he got by, gained the doorway, and crawled like a snake in the mud, disappeared and reappeared in the hundred humid mouths of the chaparral, scaled the height, descended the slope, and fell, overcome with fatigue and well-earned happiness, between his wife and child. But the night fled in a deep tomblike sleep without giving the fugitive an opportunity to savor his amorous illusions. And much before dawn, ever driven by the mayordomo's threat—"If you don't obey you'll be screwed. The patrón will kick you out of your huasipungo—" he returned racing over the mountain paths to the Rinconada woods.

Because on Sundays, in spite of the promises, the peons in the firewood and charcoal work had only half a day off, Andrés Chiliquinga's flights became very frequent. Unfortunately, one night, a night darker and rainier than usual, on arriving at his huasipungo and crossing the opening in the cactus fence he noticed something unusual: the dog, meek and silent as if he had just been punished, entwined himself in Andrés' legs, and the sadness and indifference of the hut stood out unrelievedly in the darkness. Filled with a violent unrest the Indian ran to the door of his hut. It was tied with a strand of filthy cloth.

"Cunshi . . . Cunshi . . . ," he muttered while he was opening the door.

When he entered, a feeling of pain and emptiness pierced his heart. He felt the straw mattress. He looked in the corners. He seized the cold ashes.

"Cunshiii!" he shouted in a maddened, dissonant voice.

His unanswered and unechoing calls—the night and the rain smothered everything—convinced the lover. His Cunshi was gone. So was the baby. Who could have taken them away? Who? No! She wasn't capable of fleeing by her own will. The devil of a mayordomo. The patrón as all-powerful as the Almighty Father. In the manor house . . . How to go there? How to knock? How to excuse his presence? Impossible! With a muttered oath Andrés fell on the straw mattress. He was alone, so alone that he thought he could feel the solitude. Yes. It was a thick sweat that covered his skin, that flowed from his very nerves. He tried to phrase a complaint that would relieve his asphyxia, would console him.

"Cunshi . . . Cunshi . . ."

Suddenly, in a crazy trick of his fantasy and impotence, he saw himself pummeling the invulnerable walls of the manor house with his fists. No one responded. Why? He flew to the priest and on his knees told him his story. The saintly man asked him for money to grant him Christian counsel. Tired of wandering on the roads, on the mountain paths, on . . . Tired of having knocked at all doors without any hope, he muttered again:

"Cunshi . . . Cunshi . . ."

His voice had become a soft moan, but in his mind from time to time there exploded foolish, childish ideas: "The robust woman . . . the keeper of his house . . . The guagua . . . Where could they have gone to, pes? Who had taken them away? Patrón grande, su mercé, also . . . ? The cholus? Everyone? . . . Watching the fields, the cows, the lambs, the chickens, the pigs . . . Watching everything, pes . . . Goddamit . . . Who? Who sent them away? Leaving him, the father of the family, all alone . . . Who?" And the Indian continued his questions in spite of his deep conviction that . . . the patrón, the mayordomo, the foreman, the sheriff, the priest, mistress Blanquita. Yes. Anyone who was a relative or friend of the patrón, anyone whose face was washed and knew how to read papers.

And so the hours glided over his worried stupor, a stupor that brought to the Indian the bitter and repressed conformity of those who are weak. Who was he to cry out, to question? Who was he to inquire about his family? Who was he to have feelings? An Indian. Oh! The fear of punishment, felt in every recess of his soul, in every pore in his body, heightened with his justification of his secret rebellion. Rebellion like that of a slave.

By the temperature, by the odor, by the direction of the wind that whistled through the roof, by the almost imperceptible noises, for him clear and precise, that came from the valley and from the hills, Chiliquinga estimated the time: four in the morning.

"Ave María," he exclaimed in a low voice with the terror of one who was going to be late.

He had to return to the work. His legs, his arms, his head felt like weights. But something even stronger—custom, fear—pulled him forward. The rain had let up, and, with a soft murmur, a cold wind played among the cornfields on the hillside. As he climbed the winding mountain path, in the dark dawn, which was gloomier than usual, Andrés suddenly discovered that someone—he could hear the dialogue of peons who were marching—was going through the high mountain pass. He was careful to hide in some bushes. Were they looking for him? Were they pursuing him? No! As he listened he realized what was going on. They were the Indians who formed the minga for the clearing of the big ravine—twenty or thirty shadows being driven like beasts by the whip of the mayordomo. He knew what that was. From time to time, especially in the winter months, the water backed up on the high lands, and the river bed had to be cleaned out. If this wasn't done the drainage of the thaws and the mountain storms would smash the dike which was constantly being formed by the mud, by the dislodged roots and the wastes of the hillsides, and would unleash a tragic turbid flood on the valley below—a tragic flood of diabolic force, blind, capable of destroying the irrigation system of the hacienda and of sweeping away the huasipungos along the river banks.

Andrés arrived late to work. One-Eyed Rodríguez,

with a foam of rage between his lips, after learning the truth, thanks to the investigative efficiency of his kicks and punches, admonished the Indian:

"You Indian dog! You animal! What's the idea, *pes*, of going to sleep in that pigpen of a hut instead of staying here? Here it's more sheltered, more sensible. You fool! Now you'll have to wait until I cure these Indians here who've got the shakes and chills so that you can go with them to cut down the myrtle trees."

When the morning was half gone, when the malaria victims were made whole again, dosed with beverages which were the magical secrets of the foreman, Chiliquinga entered the chaparral with them. Dazed by a strange anxiety, he plunged into his labor with a feeling of having been there always. Always. The implement like a weapon in his hands, the tree to carve at his feet like a victim, the splinters—some white, others dark—like blood and bones to aggravate the rotting humidity of the fallen leaves, the vegetation of trunks and branches twisted like the wire fences of a prison, the blows of the axes and machetes of his companions like whiplashes on his nerves, and, from time to time, a vivid recollection, painful, which seemed to come back to him after a long absence: "Cunshiii . . . You Indian dog . . . How could you leave the huasipungo abandoned? . . . The chickens, the corn, the potatoes . . . everything . . . The dog all alone, too . . . Poor Andrés Chiliquinga all alone, too . . . . ?" His thoughts more and more excited the inconsolable rage of the abandoned Indian, who in those moments was wielding the axe with a diabolic violence, with a force which at last evoked the curiosity of his companions:

"Ave María. What could it be, pes?"

"Ooof!"

"Will he bite? Will he kill?"

"Ooof!"

"If he is bewitched, we just better get out of here—but fast!"

"Ooof!"

"He can't talk?"

"Ooof!"

"With an aching heart?"

"Ooof!"

The "ooof!" of the blows on the hardness of the trunk, on the trembling of the branches, on the imprudence of the insects and the vermin, was the only answer by Andrés Chiliquinga to the questions of the Indians working around him. What could they do?

"You forward woman! Goddamit! Take this, you Indian pig, you Indian thief! I'll rip out your heart, your shit! A painful death for you, and a lousy life! Leaving the dog abandoned! Take this, take this, goddamit," the Indian repeated to himself more than once. And the splinters leaped up like white flies, like black flies, and the heart of the timber resisted his anger without being able to placate it. While he breathed, in a laboring and moaning fashion, Andrés wiped his sweat-drenched face with his hands. Then he looked about him with the misgiving of a beaten man. What could save him? Above him, the dark, heavy, and indifferent skies. Under him, the clayey muck, planting him deeper and deeper in the earth. The woodcutters around him were being ground down like animals. In the background, the wet scent of the treacherous chaparral. And tying it all together the eye of the foreman.

"Ooof!"

A long interminable hour rolled by. With a painful fatigue in his joints, Chiliquinga let himself be conquered by a drowsiness which relieved him temporarily, but when it fled from his blood and his muscles and became surprising cruel and violent, it made him shake with rage and talk and insult things—men, he couldn't:

"No . . . You won't fool me, you good-for-nothing branch, you bitchy branch, you goddam branch. Take this, take this, you scoundrel!"

In one of these rages, as he held fast with his foot the trunk that was slipping in the mud and as he delivered the accurate stroke with a demoniac lashing force, the tool, converted into a weapon by the frustrated action, narrowly missed its mark and part of the axe came to rest in the flesh and bones of the Indian's foot.

"Ouch, ouch, ayayay, goddam!"

"What's up? What's the matter?" they all asked when they heard Chiliquinga's howls.

"Ouch, ayayay, goddam!"

The troop of Indian woodcutters flocked about the injured man. Fortunately, only the point of the axe had penetrated the instep, but the flow of blood was great and it had to have attention. One Indian, doubtless the most knowledgeable in first aid, exclaimed:

"Jesus Christ! Ave María! He's really in a bad way. Someone has to go down to the ravine and fetch a little stale mud so the evil spirits don't get into the foot."

"You, boy."

"Run."

"You come back quickly, pes."

The boy chosen, a ten-year-old, barefoot, and with the face of an idiot, disappeared over a drop in the land.

"It's a shame."

"Poor Indian."

"He's losing blood, the Almighty Father's blood."

"And with a young moon, pes."

"May God keep the evil spirit from him."

During the Indians' comments, the boy who had gone for the medicine arrived with greenish and fetid mud that oozed through his fingers.

"That's good."

"Yes, taita."

"It's good and rotten," said the would-be doctor.

At that very moment One-Eyed Rodríguez arrived on the scene and furiously cried:

"Goddamit! What's going on here, pes? What are you doing, you Indian swine?"

"Nothing, patroncitu."

"What do you mean, nothing?"

"It's Andrés' foot. He really made a mess of it. It's in very bad shape."

The cholo bent over the wounded man and, after examining the case, muttered in a didactic tone, as an example and warning for the rest of them:

"Just what I was saying. Something will happen to this dirty Indian because he came here without a real will to work. Our Father above has punished you, you fool."

"Jesus, Mary . . ."

"Poor Indian, pes."

"The misfortune . . ."

The sympathetic comments of the peons were interrupted by the foreman:

"What are you going to put on it, pes?"

"This here."

"Mud? Why mud, pes? Do you think you're going to stop up a pipe? Now you'll see what I do. José Tarqui!"

"Yes, boss."

"Bring me some spider webs from the hut. You bring plenty, don't . . ."

"Yes, taiticu."

"It's like the hand of Divine Providence," the foreman said. Then, while waiting for the medicine, he addressed the wounded man and said, "And now you're not going to be able to stand, pes, you fool."

"I'll be able to, patroncitu."

"Yes, but that's not all there's to it."

"Be able to. Be able to," muttered the Indian Chiliquinga with superstitious anxiety over the blood, his blood which was staining the ground.

"You really screwed yourself."

"No. Noooo."

"Now you'll be the cripple Andrés," said the cholo with a sarcastic sadism.

With a murmur of voices and dissembled laughter, the Indian woodcutters greeted the joke of the one-eyed man who enjoyed a certain reputation for cleverness and a vulgar wit.

"Just this, that's all, pes."

"Just this . . . just this," mocked the cholo, taking the cobwebs from the Indian's hands.

"Yes, taiticu."

"It's like the hand of God. Only this will cure you, you fool," said One-Eyed Rodríguez while he applied, with the sureness and care of an experienced doctor bandaging a wound with gauze and disinfectants, the filthy cobwebs on the bleeding mouth of the wound on Chiliquinga's foot. The Indian tried to smother his pain and oaths with his teeth clenched at each pressure by the quack doctor. When the foreman thought everything was ready, he lifted his eyes to look for a strip or a rag to wrap around the precious medicine and hold it fast.

"What do you want, pes, taiticu?" asked one of the peons.

"Where's a cord?"

"A cord."

"To tie with, you fools."

"There isn't any."

"There isn't any, pes, patroncitu."

"Goddam! There isn't any . . . There isn't any . . . You miserable savages . . . You can tell them just by a little rag. When you're dying and fall into Hell's great cauldron, the Lord God will say too, 'There isn't any . . . There isn't any mercy.' "

"Holy Mary."

"Jesus."

"Where can we find it, pes?"

Without waiting to hear more, One-Eyed Rodríguez pounced on the nearest Indian, who, leaning on his axe, had been watching the scene like a transfixed sleepwalker and was unable to dodge the cholo's grabbing hand. The cholo, taking advantage of a rip already there, tore a strip from the Indian's greasy work-shirt.

A burst of laughter and interjections broke out among the Indians at the expression on the victim's face when he found himself despoiled of the rag that had covered his belly.

"Ooooh . . ."

"How ridiculous he looks."

"Goddam."

"Just look at him, pes."

"Look at the belly button."

"His belly button is bare," said someone, referring to the naked navel of the Indian who had had his shirt torn.

"His belly button is bare!" they all chorused.

At this very moment One-Eyed Rodríguez had finished the treatment. Without further delay, and with loud cracks of the whip, which restored him to his post of foreman, he imposed order on the peons.

"That's enough laughing! Back to work, you lazy dogs!"

"Ooooh . . ."

"There's still two hours before dark."

At once everything went back to the monotony of the work—throughout the width, the length, and the depth of the chaparral.

"Since you won't be able to use the axe, just go into

the ravine and gather some green leaves. We'll need them to cover the charcoal we're going to burn tomorrow," the cholo ordered, speaking to Chiliquinga who was still lying on the ground.

"Patroncitu, patroncitu," murmured the Indian, trying to get up. But when he couldn't, through too little fortitude and too much pain, the foreman helped him along with tremendous shouts and a blind rain of whiplashes.

"So you are going to act like a little baby or a pregnant woman, are you?"

"Aaaay."

"You sniveling Indian. Get up, goddamit!"

"Ayayay."

The following morning the wounded man felt as though his heart and all his pulses had lodged in his foot. Besides, he was suffering a powerful cramp in his groin. The fever burning his body evaporated the moisture from his poncho, his work-shirt, and from his denim pants, all greasy and sweaty. But habit which drives subconsciously, the foreman who was watching, and the work that awaited him made the wounded man rise.

Three days later, Chiliquinga tried to get up, moving with great difficulty. Twice, three times. Then, his will failing him, he fell back on the ground moaning like a drunkard. And when the foreman arrived, his whip lost its magic.

"Goddam! We'll have to see what's wrong with this no-good Indian. The lazy dog. He's just lazy, that's all. He's trying to . . . trying to . . . ," shouted One-Eyed Rodríguez, attempting to justify his cruelty to the wounded man. His whiplashes and kicks had no result at all.

It was then that the chorus of woodcutters who were watching dared to say:

"Poor Andrés."

"Like one bewitched."

"In the devil's power."

"Holy Mary—Ave María."

"Taiticu."

"It's the Evil One."

"The foot."

"We should really look at his foot."

And one of the Indians, the kindest and most daring, came up to the sick man and carefully undid the bandage. The filthy cloth, spotted with blood, pus, and mud, emitted a carrion stench when it was unwound.

"Oo-oo-oo . . ."

"Oh!"

When the wound was bared, everyone could see, in a devilish effervescence, a seething fabric alive with strange threads.

"It's the mountain worms."

"The mountain worms have gone into the Indian's foot."

"Arí, pes."

"Wormy like a mule's hoof."

"Just like a beast's."

"The mountain worms."

"May the Almighty Father guard him."

"Protect and favor him, pes."

"Indian animal. They'll . . . they'll have to take him down to the hacienda. Here he's no good at all . . . at all," One-Eyed Rodríguez said when confronted with the evidence.

Two Indians carried the sick man and they disappeared on the slope, leaving behind the echo of the shouts and curses of the cholo Rodríguez.

THE WOUNDED MAN's first visitor was the mayordomo of Cuchitamba, who wanted to make sure of the truth. "No one's going to make a fool of me. Least of all one of these Indian dogs," he said to himself as he entered the hut on Andrés Chiliquinga's huasipungo. Behind him came an Indian quack doctor of medium height, huddled under a poncho, with dark wrinkled face and dry nervous hands.

With a mysterious curiosity, after becoming confident in the darkness of the hut, Policarpio and the quack bent over the bundle which was the unconscious and feverish body of the sick man. And, after examining the swollen leg and smelling the wound, the Indian with the dry nervous hands stated with a voice and gesture laden with superstition:

"This . . . this . . . he seems bewitched. He is bewitched."

"Bewitched?"

"Arí, patroncitu."

"Goddam! Tricky Indian bastard. Just to get to his woman every night. Every single night. They can't make a fool of me."

"No, patroncitu. He stepped on something bad.

Something put there by the hand of the Evil Spirit."

"What crap!"

"But it's so. He's bad for a human being. He can jump like a flea."

"So, all right. You've got to cure him. That's an order from patrón grande, su mercé."

"Arí, taiticu."

"And you'll have to stay here in the hut to take care of him."

"Aw . . ."

"Cut out the 'aw.' . . . Cunshi can't come. She's suckling Señora Blanca's little baby."

"I'll go right away to the mountains and to a dark cave to gather some herbs. They'll remove the Evil Spirit. Just wait here a little while, patroncitu, until I come back. It's a good idea to protect yourself with the sign of the cross."

"Oh? I'll wait for you. Come back soon."

"Arí, patroncitu."

When the mayordomo was alone with the sick man, who was ranting like one possessed, he felt a cloying fear crawl up his legs and his arms. "He's bewitched . . . bewitched," he thought, recalling the mysterious voice and the dramatic gesture of the quack. "He can leap, he can jump like a flea, goddamit," he said to himself, panic-stricken, and dashed out of the hut looking for his mule. They weren't going to screw him like that. And when he was on the beast trotting along one of the paths that led to the hacienda, he muttered in a low voice:

"Bewitched. Who would have thought it? Not even the priest knows about that. Those Indian dogs are the devil's own sons."

Of the voices which succeeded in penetrating the sick man's subconscious mind, cutting through his fever and pain, only one remained sticking like a dagger in his

throat, like a crude knife scraping his heart: Cunshi . . .
Cunshiii.

When the quack, laden with herbs, returned, he
found Chiliquinga rolling on the bare earth floor of the
hut, repeating:

"Cunshiii! You hussy! My darling!"

" 'You hussy, my darling!' May Taita Dios protect
you. May Taita Dios defend you," repeated the dark and
wrinkle-faced Indian, leaping on the sick man in order to
hold him by force while he said strange prayers over him
—prayers to drive away and conquer the demons which
had bewitched Chiliquinga. Then, when Andrés calmed
down, he made a fire on the hearth with dried cow dung
and dry branches and, in an earthen pot which Cunshi
used for cooking the porridge, prepared a brew with all
the different ingredients he had brought from the ravine.
While he kindled the flame, and just as the water started
to sing of boiling, the Indian, skillful demon fighter,
began to quiver, and contorted his wrinkled immutable
face in a fierce grimace. He mumbled some words of his
own invention, rubbed his chest, his armpits, his groin,
and his temples with a lodestone and a piece of lignum-
vitae wood which he wore about his neck. When the
mysterious brew was ready, he dragged the sick man like
a bale of hay to the hearth, took his swollen foot,
pulled off the bandage, and on the wound—which was
dripping with worms and greenish pus—he clamped an
absorbent, voracious kiss, like that of a leech. The
wounded man shrieked as he twisted convulsively, vehe-
mently, but the sucking lips of the quack sank deeper
and deeper into his work, even though the quack could
feel on his gums, on his tongue, on his palate, and even in
his throat, a sticky tickling with a sickening stench and a
taste like the rotting scum of the swamp. The pain and
spasms of the sick man soon emerged in a deafening

scream which left him motionless and rendered him unconscious. Then the sucking of the quack became stronger and stronger, and a glint of triumph lit his eyes. He was certain; he knew it was the same with everyone bewitched: when the demons left the body they always strangled the victim's consciousness.

The able disenchanter emptied his mout. i with a spit which he bestowed on the fire in the hearth. Black and smelly smoke climbed along the wall tapestried with soot.

"It's very easy to smell the singed tail of the devil," said the quack watching the saliva, bloody pus, and worms boil in the fire. Meanwhile, with the back of his shirtsleeve, he wiped away the vestiges of thick dribble that still clung to his lips. Then, taking advantage of Chiliquinga's unconscious state, he immersed the wounded foot by holding it in both hands in the still steaming brew. Content with his work, he muttered at last:

"You can't fool around with me, you big red devil. And now I have to keep alert until he's better."

With the corn, the barley flour, beef suet, and some potatoes which he found in the hut, the quack fed himself and the sick man and the dog.

He had to repeat the same operation for a week to disinfect the wound, and another week of bandaging was required for the wound to begin to heal. Nevertheless, Andrés Chiliquinga remained a cripple as predicted by One-Eyed Rodríguez. This defect lowered his value as a worker tremendously, but Don Alfonso Pereira's charity and Señora Blanquita's kind sentiments allowed the Indian to stay on in his huasipungo. And the nicest and most generous part of all was that they allowed him to watch the crops, to become a chacracama, during his convalescence.

"He'll just have to spend the days and nights looking

after the big field. Any eight-year-old Indian boy can do it. But since the Indian dog had that bad luck, we'll have to help him until he is recovered or until we decide what to do with him. I only hope . . ."

"He'll remain a cripple, I believe, patrón," put in the mayordomo.

"Then we'll . . ."

"Ah! We'll have to keep him until his woman weans my baby. Her milk agrees with him. Why not admit it? After so much suffering. She's good . . . that woman is really good," said Pereira's wife.

"Yes, very good," said Don Alfonso, suppressing a mocking itching of his sexual desire for the Indian woman, of his lust which he kept hidden and lying in ambush. Her splendid breasts, her thick lips, her elusive eyes, ah!

Andrés Chiliquinga was in a hut perched on stilts in the middle of an enormous cornfield, where the night wind whistled through the leaves with a metallic sound. At times he rose on his good foot, with his arms outstretched like a scarecrow; at other times he dragged himself like a worm across the raised floor of the hut. He practiced at all hours his best shouts, some hoarse, some high-pitched, most of them extended, in order to banish the hungry birds and cattle.

"Eaaaa . . . !"

"Aaaa . . . !" from the horizon came an answering echo riding on the crests of the sea of corn.

One night, it must have been very late, the Indians from the huasipungos on the nearest hill heard a rush of hoofbeats thundering into the valley. It was the hacienda's cattle, which, breaking down their fence, had poured through the opening in search of a feast of corn.

Then, from the silence and the darkness, rose long horrendous shouts:

"Look out . . ."

"Guard the hacienda!"

"Look out for the cattle!"

"They're in the big cornfield!"

"Guard the haciendaaa!"

"Look out . . ."

The voices, ringing with horror and sudden pain, somersaulted down the valley after the cattle. They leaped from the hill, from the low hilltop, from all sides.

Andrés Chiliquinga, maddened by the hullabaloo, jumped among the furrows. His lameness kept him from running, chaining him to fear, to a lack of confidence.

"Goddam . . . goddam," he repeated in order to enrage himself and to temper the pain of his helplessness.

His struggle was long and desperate. Sometimes crawling, sometimes jumping, he evaded the blind charges of the cattle with his body, which became a nervous rag. Finally, availing himself of sticks, stones, handfuls of dirt, shouts, oaths, curses, and threats he chased out the cattle scattered among the corn.

That unusual racket woke Don Alfonso, who, with the arrogance and heroism of a general in the field, threw on his poncho and went out on the porch half-dressed.

"What's the matter?" his wife and daughter asked from their beds.

"Nothing. Some foolishness. Don't you two get up. I'll go out wherever . . . I'll . . ."

Once he went into action, he awoke the servants and, on learning what had happened, mobilized all the hacienda household and ordered them to march to the rescue of the caretakers, to the rescue of Andrés Chiliquinga.

"The cripple probably can't move about. It was stupid to use him as a chacracama. I said it was stupid."

When he was left alone, leaning against one of the porch pillars, his glance and imagination both lost in the infinite darkness, he thought for a long time in a schoolboy way about the heroic feat he had just accomplished. Yes, really. The deed he had just done. He believed it something unheard of to have gotten up at midnight just to save his crops; that was Indians' work, not his. Ah! His spirit of self-sacrifice . . . He really had plenty to brag about now, chatting at his club, attending meetings over a cup of chocolate, at the gatherings of the Agricultural Society. And how would he really tell it? Because after all he . . . he knew how . . . The oppressive and unnerving blackness of the wild night; the very kingdom of souls in purgatory. He would naturally exaggerate, in his own favor, the fierceness of the animals and the anxiety of the Indians' cries.

"No . . . One shouldn't get too involved in these deep affairs because one can get caught," he muttered to himself. But his pride and omnipotence at the same time were thinking: "I am the chief of a mass of workers. The flaming torch. Without me, there would be nothing in this whole damned region."

And as he was returning to his room looking for a reward, for a happy, savory relaxation, his mind evoked, with loathing, the naked, deformed and flabby body of Doña Blanca. "When she was young. Ah! What year was it? . . . Boy . . . So much fucking! So many visits to the sacristy." Suddenly he remembered the Indian wetnurse who was sleeping in the corner room, a few paces away. "Goddam . . . of course . . . I can do it," he told himself as he put his ear to the keyhole of her room. A light snoring sound and an odor of soiled clothes aroused his youthful ardor. Nervous and trembling, he rubbed his hands together. "Nobody . . . nobody will know . . ." And then he thought: "And what if it's found out? How shameful! Shameful? Why? They have all done it." Besides, wasn't he used to seeing, and proving, ever since his boyhood that all the Indian servant girls were outraged, raped, and deflowered as a matter of course by the patrones? He was a patrón grande, su mercé! He was master of everything, of the Indian woman, too. He softly pushed open the door. In the blackness of the room, blacker than the night itself, Don Alfonso advanced, groping his way. He advanced up to, and on top of, the woman who tried to straighten up on her humble straw bed at the foot of the baby's cradle. She tried to call for help, to breathe. Unfortunately the patrón's voice and weight undid all her efforts. On top of her, trembling anxiously and with a violent lust, was pressing the being who, in her mind, was confused with the priest's threats, with the authority of the sheriff, and with the very face of Taita Dios. Nevertheless, the Indian Cunshi, perhaps moved by the bad advice of an instinctive impulse, tried to avoid him, tried to save herself. But it was useless. The large imperious hands of the man raked her body cruelly, crushed her with a strange entreating violence. Rendered motionless, conquered, she let him have his way. But she closed her eyes and became rigid as a corpse. It was the master who could do anything he wanted in that region. Shout? Who would hear her? The Indian Andrés, her husband? "Oh, the poor helpless cripple," Cunshi thought with a tenderness that brought tears to her eyes.

"Shake it, you Indian bitch," Pereira cried in a low voice, enraged by the female's passiveness. He had expected undoubtedly a greater pleasure, more . . .

"Aaay."

"Shake it up."

Shout? So that they'd throw her man off the huasipungo. So the patron's wife and daughter could see her forwardness, her robust build? What for? No! That she wouldn't do! It was better to stay silent, without feeling.

"Shake it up."

"Aaay."

She was forced to dam the bitterness that was bursting in her breast; she had to swallow the tears that were trickling down her nose.

When the patrón got up and felt his way to the door, he said half aloud:

"They are like animals. They don't give you the enjoyment you should get. They make love like cows. It's easy to see . . . They are an inferior race."

When he was figuring, on the next day, the amount of damage the cattle had done in the big field, he asked the mayordomo:

"How many stalks did they knock down?"

"I counted around two hundred, patrón."

"That's worth about . . ."

"Thirty sucres, roughly."

"Well, charge it to the account of that Indian rogue."

"That's what we'll do, su mercé."

WHEN CUNSHI RETURNED to the huasipungo, Andrés cast sly glances at her belly. Was she? Or wasn't she? She, on her part, understanding his bitter misgiving, tried to remove his suspicion by fearlessly letting him see her lean belly.

Toward the middle of summer, the roads good once again, Doña Blanca and Lolita decided to return to the capital. They thought all their problems were solved; the family honor was once more immaculately shining. Doña Blanquita's maternal feeling was more tenderly and more restlessly revived. Only Don Alfonso still was in some difficulty. He didn't know how to phrase his apologies to his uncle and to the firms with whom he had dealt and contracted the exploitation of the timber, of the petroleum, of . . . whatever there might be.

"Don't fret so much," his wife consoled him when he told her of his problems.

"But what will I say to them?"

"Exactly what you've done. You couldn't do more with the little money they gave you."

"So little . . ."

"You bought the Oriente mountains."

"But what about the road?"

"Let them build it."

"Woman, you know darn well I'll have to do it."

"Let them give you some more money."

"More . . ."

"It's logical."

"And then there's the huasipungos."

"That'll be easier."

"Easier?"

"Of course, hombre. You come with us. You speak to those gentlemen. You say this to them. Nothing more could be done. And so . . . And if they agree, you come back alone and begin the tasks. We'll . . ."

"Sí, I see."

"Do you want to bury us in this inferno? Lolita must start over."

"Start over."

"And my baby. His upbringing, his education."

"You're right. Sí . . . There's no other way."

"Nothing else can be done."

What Doña Blanca really yearned for was to return to the capital, to the gossip of her snobbish friends—a mafia of presumptuous and predatory half-breeds—to the novenas of the Virgin of Pompeya, to the jewels, to Father Uzcátegui. And she had her way. Unfortunately, Don Alfonso was not permitted to enjoy his stay in the capital. His uncle Julio's advice and threats on the one hand and the gringos' plans and money on the other—generosity measured out with an eyedropper—buried him once more in the country.

Don Alfonso Pereira came into Tomachi at twilight. When he arrived at the sheriff's house Juana was, as usual, on the porch selling fermented cane juice and beef entrail soup to some ten Indians who were eating and drinking seated on the ground. On seeing the patrón of Cuchitambo the woman exclaimed:

"Hi, there! You have come back."

"My dear Juana."

"Good evening."

"And how are you and Jacinto?"

"Just fine. Jacintooo! Our dear patrón is here!"

"Again . . ."

"You came alone?"

"Quite alone."

"You're a bachelor, then."

"A bachelor."

"I see, pes. Too bad."

At that very moment Jacinto Quintana appeared through one of the porch doors, left his cigarette butt on a stone seat, and with a servile, silly gesture, a specialty of his wide, greasy simpleton face, said to the recent arrival:

"Why not dismount and stay a while, pes, patrón?"

"Ah!"

"Have a cinammon with brandy. It's good for the ailments of the páramo."

"Stay a little while," put in the woman.

"Thank you. Thanks a lot," said Pereira as he dismounted. Then he continued:

"It would be a good idea to send somebody to the priest to tell him to join us because I want to chat with him and invite him to a drink."

"O.K., pes."

"Whatever you say, patrón. Right away," said the cholo, wishing to go into the house. But his wife, half-grumbling, half-flattering, interrupted:

"What's this, pes? Come in first and sit down, rest a while."

"Of course. Come in . . . come in, patrón."

The cholo Quintana installed Don Alfonso in the room that served as a bedroom for the family. It was a dark room with a mat, with the walls covered with time-yellowed illustrations from newspapers and magazines. At the head of a bed of perilous architecture, overly wide—the whole family slept in it—there was an altar to the Virgin of the Spoon held on by nails and pins. There were also ornamental wreaths and decorative flowers made of colored paper and pictures of saints with pharmaceutical ads. An effluvium of recent hangovers and old saddles saturated the atmosphere. Filth crouched in the corners and under the furniture.

"Just sit down, patrón," invited the cholo as he wiped off a rustic bench with the corner of his poncho.

"Sit here . . . It's better," proposed the woman caressing a spot on the bed.

"Sí, it's better here," concluded Don Alfonso giving preference to the woman.

"It's O.K. there, too."

"This is better . . . If I get drunk I won't be needing anything."

"Nothing."

"But what do you want to get drunk on, pes?" asked the female.

"Ah! No one knows," said Pereira with a tight little smile of succulent anticipation.

"Jesus!" exclaimed Juana roguishly, and went out through the door that led to the porch.

"Pardon me, patrón. I'll tell the boy to go after the priest," said Jacinto disappearing in his turn.

A few minutes later, the woman returned with a plate filled with tortillas of potato and stewed corn, all sprinkled with chili and chopped lettuce. And with false humility she offered it to him:

"A little something for an appetizer, pes."

"Marvelous!" exclaimed the proprietor of Cuchi-tambo, eyeing the succulent and appetizing food.

"Do you want a little corn liquor? I'm asking because as you . . ."

"Ah!"

"Pes, not the chicha for the Indians fermented from cactus juice. The real stuff. Made with Indian corn."

"I'd prefer a little beer. A couple of bottles."

"We have only the Lona brand. The other kind ferments too quickly."

"Whatever you have. This chili is kind of hot . . ."

"You'll probably also want a little brandy to wake up your mouth."

"A fourth of a bottle. The priest will be here any minute."

The parson arrived a half hour later. His appearance introduced a familiar and noisy note into the conversation, the unequal dialogue between the landowning patrón and the cholo sheriff.

"What's new in our capital city, Don Alfonso?"

"Nothing."

"How about the turmoil. Has the government fallen yet?"

"No. Why should it . . . ?"

"How are the women?" insisted the cassocked-one cynically.

"Same as always," said Pereira, and in an authoritative voice called the sheriff's wife to ask for another quarter of a bottle of brandy. She objected:

"With taita curita you'll need a whole bottle."

"O.K. A whole one."

Scarcely had the bottle arrived when Don Alfonso, with a generous pomposity, began to share the liquor with his friends, calling Juana to have a glass from time to time. She never took part in the serious, profound conversation of the men, but she liked to drink moderately.

The sincerity, passions, and the fantasy of the three men's dialogue rose on wings of alcohol. The patrón, the priest, and the law. Don Alfonso—the imperious gesture, the tremulous voice, the hard, firm, threatening look, the pantomime of the hands—brought up the problem of the road with his friends:

"We three are the only ones who can carry out this great work which has been needed for many centuries."

"We?" said the priest in a questioning tone that disclosed his feeling of helplessness.

"That is . . ."

"And who else, goddamit? Many are called but few are chosen. You from the pulpit, Señor priest, and you, Jacinto, from the sheriff's office."

"How, pes?" the cholo dared to inquire.

"The thing is to begin at once this titanic labor. The fatherland demands it, requests it, needs it!" shrieked the owner of Cuchitambo, putting an irrefutable fervor in his words.

"Aha!" exclaimed the cassocked one.

"Sííí, pes," the sheriff sighed.

"We must use all the able-bodied people in town. Every single one! I'll donate the Indians. With a minga of four or five weeks' duration we'll have the best road in the world, goddamit. The Minister . . . has personally offered to send me an engineer and some equipment if the road is to be built."

"Then the thing is settled," said the friar.

"That's the only way, pes," said the cholo.

"That's the only way this nation will take a definite step toward civilization and progress."

"The only way," they all agreed.

"Let's drink . . . Let's drink a little snort to our happy beginning," said Pereira, thrilled by the prospect of a victory.

"Your health."

"Your health, my dear priest. And yours, patrón."

"Your health!"

After a short pause the landowner went on, and with a sudden movement of his hand, gave a flourish to the sentence he must have heard from the lips of some political demagogue:

"The time has come to give life and culture to the inhabitants of this fair region! Roads . . . roads are the very life of towns, and towns must build their roads."

"How beautiful!" exclaimed the sheriff, fascinated by the words.

"Sí, that's right. But I wonder if we can build twenty kilometers of road, which is what we need, with only the mingas," said the priest, tilting his hat over one ear.

"Then you, my dear friend, don't know that the San Gabriel road was constructed largely in that way."

"Sí?"

"So it is, pes."

"And today that area has improved 50 per cent in everything. For a small hacienda, a piece of land without water, without anything, they have just offered a relative of mine fifty thousand sucres."

"That's really so, pes."

"And the road would increase the importance of all the parishes in this region," murmured the cassocked one, as if speaking to himself.

"Not just in this region, in the whole province."

"And the sheriffs' offices would be well supplied, pes."

"Of course!"

"Your health, my dear priest. And yours, patrón."

"Your health!"

"Then you two will join in our great task?"

"We will!"

"I only hope that your present patriotism isn't just brought on by the alcohol," said Don Alfonso Pereira in a threatening tone.

"How can you think such a thing?" answered the priest indignantly.

"Yes, how, pes?" echoed Quintana.

A single idea was becoming an obsession with the priest: "When the mingas are begun I'll hold a solemn mass with five or six sponsors, with vespers, a sung mass, a sermon . . .What the hell! And we'll hold another one when the work is over to show our thanks . . ."

"We can begin as soon as possible," said the owner of Cuchitambo.

"In summer. After the feast of the Virgin of the Spoon."

"Whatever you say, my dear priest. Whenever you wish," said Don Alfonso, winking an eye roguishly.

"No. It's not of myself I'm thinking. I said that because in that way the Indians and peasants will feel protected by the Most Holy Virgin and so work with greater zest."

"Work their asses off," interrupted the cholo Jacinto with a naïve sincerity.

Without considering the sheriff's inopportune remark Don Alfonso said jokingly:

"You rogue of a priest. What you really want is not to be hurt by the big fiesta."

"And so what?" asked the priest with unexpected cynicism.

"I get it. One or two months of recuperation, eh? That's how . . . That's how you can have another one dedicated to the mingas."

"It wouldn't be a bad idea."

"Bad, no. One hundred sucres from each sponsor for the mass."

"Nothing is done on this earth without some help."

"Nothing . . . It's true. Just so the sponsors aren't from my hacienda."

"Ah, they'd have to be in on it."

"Now you've gone and screwed me, goddamit."

"You can't build a road out of thin air, my dear friend."

"No. Of course you can't . . ."

"With this little business your property will double in value."

"More than that," said Pereira, with the same cynicism that had shielded the priest.

The sheriff's stupefied pause in those brief instants while absorbing, imbued with patriotic curiosity and faith, the sage chatter of the other two men, exploded in an urgent complaint. How much would be in it for him?

"And what about me? How can I help, pes?"

"You . . . You'll be the collector."

"And what is that, pes?"

"You'll reap what the priest sows."

"I don't understand."

"You'll corral the cattle prepared by the sermons in the church."

"Oh! I thought there was something for me."

"As the supreme authority of the town."

"As the man who is trusted."

"As the patriot . . ."

"Sí, now I get it . . ."

"You're to get them all to work whether they want to or not."

"All by myself?"

"We must make our move at the right time. A fair, for example."

"Just as they come out from mass."

"Your health, my dear priest. Yours too, patrón."

"To your health!"

When the chola Juana came in with the last bottle of brandy she could find in her store, Don Alfonso asked his allies:

"How many do you think will show up willingly to work on the road?"

"Well . . ."

"Probably . . ."

"How many, goddamit?" insisted the owner of Cuchitambo with his inquisitive eyes revealing a dangerous alcoholic obsession.

"Plenty, pes."

"Many, Don Alfonsito."

"How many?"

"As many as you want."

"As many . . ."

"Goddam! That's no answer. How many?"

"Your health, patrón Alfonsito. Yours, dear priest."

"To your health!"

At that moment the sheriff's wife illuminated the drunkenness of the men with a tallow candle standing in an empty bottle.

"How many? Count them for me!"

"O.K. More than a hundred."

"That's right. Over a hundred."

"Count them for me, goddamit!" demanded the landowner, twisting his mouth into a grimace of mockery and anger.

The priest and the cholo sheriff, seeing that the situation was deteriorating, did their best to remove Pereira's crazy obsession by enumerating the possible workers, those who should go, those who . . . In their abused chaotic minds, at once perceptive and absurd, rose the figures of the local people. Old Calupiña; Melchor Santos and his two good-looking daughters; Cuso, the telegraph operator who lived in a hut on the slope; Timoteo Mediavilla, the schoolteacher—the mockery and the scourge of the good priest's cocks; the noisy guy who complained of an aching back; the maker of fibre sandals;

the young Indian who had been a cop in Quito and who had to return to the village because he had gotten into some sort of mess with the Police Inspector's cook; One-Armed Conchambay; limping Amador; One-Eyed Rodríguez; Luis Mendieta; the Ruata brothers . . .

"And who else?" insisted the drunken landowner.

"To your health, patrón. And yours, dear priest."

"Your health!"

"Who else?"

"The chola Miche with her swarm of kids," exclaimed the priest in a tone of happy discovery.

"Of course . . ."

"And who else?"

"Cat-Eyes with his wife and the zambo cousin who has arrived with some merchandise from up the mountain."

"From up the mountain, pes."

"Who else?"

"Grandfather Juan . . . The Indians from the Caltahuano páramo."

"And who else, I say?"

"The school kids."

"The children!"

"We need more, goddamit!" insisted Don Alfonso, banging on the table. The bottles jumped, the glasses and the candle went flying in a hiccup of fright. Such an unheard of attitude spread terror in the lapels of God's representative and in the poncho of the agent of the law.

"But Don Alfonso . . ."

"Patrón . . ."

"I said we need more, goddamit," again insisted the lord of the area, pursuing the problem to the embarrassment of his friends and allies, who, with fear and prudence mingled in their countenances, forced themselves to try to smile.

"We do?"

"Ha . . . ha . . . ha . . ."

A dangerous pause developed. Don Alfonso threw across the table into the evasive face of the priest and into the humble smile of the cholo sheriff—like a flaming coal, challengingly—a mute, but authoritative question which smouldered in his eyes with a threatening, alcoholic glitter. The landowner was distressed by the stupidity of his allies. How could they not imagine to whom he was referring? Who were, in reality, the decisive men in realizing his plan to drill through the mountains, to drain the marshes, to conquer the páramo, to complete a project which not even the government itself could do, even though at times aided by the priests of the Almighty Father and at other times allied with the devils of the liberals. Wearying of awaiting a reply, the master of Cuchitambo shouted:

"And what about you two? You don't count? Wise guys, goddamit!"

"Naturally. That's understood."

"Of course, pes."

"We'll lead them all."

"In front of them all."

"That's what I wanted to hear you say . . . from your own lips. . . . You were being stupid . . . but . . ." concluded the landowner with a triumphant air ending a game which had become not at all pleasing.

"That we took for granted," said the friar, again breathing peacefully.

"For granted, pes."

With euphoric joy, after noting that the brandy had been drained from the bottles, Don Alfonso Pereira got to his feet and shouted to the mistress of the house:

"Juanaaa!"

"What do you want, pes, patrón?" Jacinto intervened obsequiously.

"Some more brandy. Just another little bottle."

"But there is no more, patrón. We've drunk it all, every single drop, pes," said the sheriff.

"Almost two bottles," said the priest.

"But . . . No. We can't stay here like this, just a little high," the landowner protested in a tone that admitted no argument.

"Good . . . That . . ."

"That's what I say, too, but there isn't any more, pes. Almost always we just have two bottles in the store. Only during fiestas or other occasions. . . . Now we have beer, corn liquor . . ."

"Oh, that's crud. I can fix us up. I, myself. Go, Jacinto . . . You'll have to do me a favor."

"Just tell me what you want."

"Take my mule who must be around outside."

"Ahhh! Uh-huh."

"By trotting you can reach the hacienda. Tell Policarpio in my name—he's probably expecting me—to give you a couple of bottles that I keep in the dining room cabinet."

"A couple?"

"Yes, two. Tell him to let you bring them. They contain cognac."

"Cognac!" echoed the priest, his eyes glinting thirstily.

"I'm off in a jiffy."

When the sheriff had gone off—as though fired from a gun, and the priest and the lord of Cuchitambo were alone, they exchanged an odd, knowing, little smile as they listened with satisfaction to the fading sound of the mule's hooves in the night. Then with a very frank gesture, mutually understood, they proclaimed their vile proposal to each other. It was the same old: "About an hour to get there and back. The chola woman is good, generous, and co-operative . . . What are we waiting for?" Don Alfonso, the bolder one, winked lewdly at the priest, pointing to the door through which one could arrive at the kitchen where Juana was to be found. They got to their feet like polished gentlemen: only a note of swaying, comic mockery betrayed the intoxication underlying the eager sureness and the ardent intention of the two men. They advanced one step, two steps. No . . . No, there was no reason to pounce on the prey like vultures. Everything had its limit, its style . . . "Why knock each other down for such a stupid reason? Impossible. We're friends, allies . . . ," Don Alfonso said to himself, yielding the lead to the cassocked one with a polite and gallant bow which seemed to say: "You go in first . . . Go in . . ." With a silly smile of beatific humility the priest replied: "Not at all. You . . . You first, Don Alfonsito . . ."

In the kitchen, which was lighted with a candle stuck to the wall by the stickiness of its own tallow, the chola was nodding, seated by the fire in a stove on the floor. The reflection of the flames lent a sort of trembling glow to her rosy cheeks and her half-closed eyes. The illustrious drunkard stumbled as he drew near her.

"Ave María. You almost scared me," muttered the woman lazily rubbing her eyes.

"How could I scare you, my dear little chola?" the landowner asked indulgently as he dropped down beside her.

"You're not going to begin your old tricks, are you? Jacinto . . . ," she said in a threatening tone that sought to hide a chronic adultery.

"He's not here. I sent him to the hacienda," said Don Alfonso, sliding his hands beneath the woman's skirts.

"What is it, pes?" protested Juana without moving away, letting him . . .

"My dear little chola."

"It'll be the same as always."

"The same?"

"Just until your desire passes. You promise . . . You promise . . ."

"Come on, you little fool. Wait . . . Wait . . . ," stammered the lord of Cuchitambo, his trembling hands fondling the most intimate parts of the chola woman who exuded an odor of mingled sweat and onions.

"Then . . . What was it you said, pes? What was it you promised, pes?"

"Ahah!" exclaimed Pereira, and murmured something in the ear of the woman, who at that critical point of the amorous dialogue discovered herself stretched out on her back, her skirts raised above her hips, her legs in a shameless display.

"This is what you always say and . . . ," she managed to say half smothered by the slobbering kisses and the violent caresses of the illustrious drunkard. At the crucial moment she was always weak. How many times hadn't she promised herself that she'd demand something? Demand, in exchange for her body, a little of all she had wanted since she was a little girl. To demand of the only man who could give it to her: what she needed for her children, for her home, to dress herself like a señora from the city, to eat . . . He never kept his word . . . Never! But nevertheless, he made her dream. Dream ever since the first time. She'd never forget the first time. She had screamed and defended herself with her fists, with her teeth. Ah! But he . . . He crushed her breasts, her belly, he kissed her cheeks, her ears, her neck, paying no attention to her blows. Then he threw her to the ground in a field of clover and dug his knees between her legs. And she . . . She could have kept up her defense, perhaps conquered and fled. But, suddenly he spoke to her with a passionate tenderness which seemed to be real of things that no one had ever said to her: "I'll leave my wife and marry you. I'll give you a cow. I'll take you to Quito. You'll be the mistress of Cuchitambo." Confronted by such affection and by a glimpse of an unattainable paradise all her feminine scruples drained from the chola's soul, and all her wrath melted in a flood of tears of mingled entreaty and pleasure. She let him have his way. Some soporific overwhelmed her with sweet hopes.

As soon as the landowner had finished, the priest came in. He, too, the minister of Taita Dios, had his way with the sheriff's wife, who could never deny him anything. Juana liked that mysterious scent of the sacristy that the tonsured one emitted at the most intimate moments. And that evening, with inciting blushes and roguishness as she found herself being caressed and desired, she objected:

"Jesús, you two must think I am a font of holy water."

"Sí . . . Sí, my little beauty . . . ," the friar murmured with difficulty, befuddled by the alcohol and his lust.

When her illustrious riders had left her, Juana got up, without much remorse; perhaps a sin with a patrón and a priest was not really a sin. But then, as she lowered her skirts over her nudity and arranged her blouse, and as she noted that her smallest son, from a shadowy corner of the kitchen had been observing the scene with eyes filled with pained surprise, she felt a shame deeper than the possible remorse, crueler than any vengeance her husband could mete out.

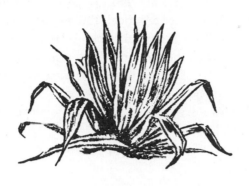

SINCE HIS CONVERSATION with his uncle Julio and since, once in the country, he had learned how fast the money came and went, Don Alfonso Pereira extended his greed over all affairs, big and small: over the projects of farm exploitation, over anything he could acquire in his role of "patrón grande, su mercé." This was undoubtedly why, when he would mount his favorite black mule to visit the village each morning to further his intrigues and labors for the community road-building, his imagination would weave long views of fruitful economic results: "I can squeeze all I want from my land, it's mine . . . From the Indians, they're mine . . . The villagers . . . Well . . . They aren't mine, but they'll do what I say, goddamit." Then he would plan to transport crops to the capital by the new road, and by train. His fancy previewed the events to come: the drilling of the mountain, the conquering of the cliff, the draining of the marsh, and, on the slopes and in the valley, the planting of gigantic cultivated fields. He also occasionally would enjoy in anticipation the pride of paying off his debt to his uncle Julio, of seeing himself as the only partner, active and effective, of the gringo gentlemen, or even of doing the whole business himself.

"But all by myself! No. Impossible! *They* know how. *They* have the practice, the experience, the machines," he reflected mentally before that daring temptation. And when he had need to visit the capital for projects, contracts, signatures, tools, money, credit, or technical help, he told Policarpio:

"By my return I must find all the slopes ploughed and planted."

"But the yoked oxen can't work on such sloping terrain, pes."

"Yes, I know. The poor beasts would roll down that slope. But that's what the Indians are for. With iron bars and picks."

"Indians on that whole slope?"

"Hell, yes!"

"But, patrón, it can't be done next week."

"Why not?"

"I'll have to go clean out the river bed. Me, in person, pes. I'll need at least twenty Indians."

"That you can take care of later."

"Impossible. What if it becomes clogged? That would be dangerous."

"Oh!"

"We must not tamper with the ways of Taita Dios."

"Goddam! That will be done later, I told you."

"O.K., pes."

"I'll spend about two weeks in the city. I've got to resolve with the Ministry the question of the engineers for the road."

"That's what I've heard, patrón. It looks like the affair is quite advanced in the town."

"I sure hope so."

"As for the cultivated fields that you—su mérce—mention . . . It would be better to use up the land in the valley, pes."

"We'll use that, too. But it's only a small area. While on the other hand, the hills . . ."

"Jesus Christ!"

Moved by an impulse of friendly confidence, a result of the insecurity and doubt of the first steps of an enterprise as tremendous as his, Don Alfonso concluded:

"I'm up to my eyebrows in debt. Nobody ever can understand another person's troubles, my dear Policarpio."

"That's the way it is, patrón."

"And these Indian pigs have seized the most fertile lands on both river banks for their huasipungos."

"That's how it has always really been."

"Goddam. By next year they'll have to clear out of that whole area and build their huts on the hilltops. This isn't the first time I've told them. This isn't the first time I've ordered them to move."

"And who is going to take their lands away, pes?"

"I am, goddamit!"

"Yeah?"

"What's that?"

"No, it's nothing, su mercé," the cholo excused himself, realizing that he had gone too far in his frankness.

"They have always thought I was their mamma and daddy. Who do these stupid Indians think I am?"

"They think just that, pes."

"Goddamit."

"The late patrón, your father, also tried to move them out. He almost was able to. The dirty Indians rebelled."

A bitter uneasiness came over the lord of Cuchitambo, foreseeing, with a bilious despair, the downfall of his omnipotence as a great landowner. He had known how difficult it would be to meet the demands of the gringo businessmen and of his uncle Julio. Despoiling the Indians of their filthy old hovels was as hard as, or harder than, pulling up a forest by the roots. And eager to put aside all future obstacles and contradictions, he exclaimed:

"Shit! They can't horse around with me!"

"Of course, they can't, su mercé," the mayordomo muttered, filled with fear and surprise at his master's rage.

"They can't . . . They can't . . ." But how could he do it? "How, goddamit?" mused Don Alfonso, echoing his own words. Happily, on this occasion—where there had always been an impenetrable fog—a ray of hope broke through. God had been good to him. He murmured in Policarpio's ear:

"Damn it! Now . . . Now I've got it."

"What is it, pes, patrón?" asked the cholo Policarpio without fully understanding the master's meaning.

"We must simply forget to clean out the river bed, eh? Just forget. Do you see? There are more practical and lucrative things to attend to," said the owner of Cuchitambo with a devilish but stupified glint in his eyes.

"Sí, patrón," muttered the mayordomo, not daring to believe that . . .

"That's how we'll solve all our problems. Every single one, damn it!"

"That's how, pes."

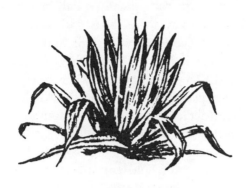

T HE RUATA BROTHERS, by order of the priest, their
spiritual leader, organized a patriotic gathering for
the community road-building project. The meetings took
place nightly in the back room of Jacinto's liquor store.
Quite often the informal sessions of the enthusiastic towns-
people wound up in drunken orgies of a violent nature,
which instead of discrediting the seriousness of the gathering brought it prestige and popularity among the resi-
dents of the whole region. The peasants then came without suspicion—from highland, lowland, table-land, valley,
jungle—spent their pennies on brandy, and offered their
experience as advice for the work on the community
project. Almost always there were cards bet on the first
drinks. The card playing quartet usually consisted of the
two Ruata brothers, Jacinto Quintana, and some easy
mark who occasionally turned out to be just the opposite.

Also, after each mass the priest spoke at length to
the faithful about the gigantic labor that was so sorely
needed and shamelessly offered generous rewards in
future bliss:

"Oh, yes! A hundred, a thousand days' indulgence
for every meter built. Only by advancing the work will
the Divine Maker bestow his greatest blessings on our
town."

His flock—both the peasants (half-breeds who were arrogant because they wore shoes and were half white) and the Indians (covered with filth and crawling with lice)—was shaken to its very core on hearing of the greater blessings and the indulgences. Then they . . . They were important people in the eyes of the Almighty Father. He was concerned. He knew . . . After all, what was the work on the road project? Nothing at all. A custom, an opportunity to get together, to be somebody. Generally, the priest's sermons would end by evoking everything that concerned his own personal interest:

"Since the feast of the Virgin didn't turn out very well, we'll have another one before the road-building starts. Don Isidro Lugo will be the sponsor for the village, and for the country we'll have the following natives: Juan Cabascango of the riverbank, Melchor Montaquisa from Cerro Chico, and Manuel Chambayacu from Guanujo."

And there was a one-hundred sucre mass, with music by the town band, with fireworks, skyrockets, and balloons at the church door. There were elegantly dressed peasants with their very best ponchos and children costumed as angels, with tin wings, their hair arranged in ill-made curls and wearing shoes. There was also a lot of incense smoke and flowers stripped of leaves to be tossed at the Virgin in the procession, a long-winded sermon, and the usual assortment of asphyxiating odors.

That same day, beginning at four in the morning, the throngs overflowed into the plaza from every street to mingle confidently at the fair—a bumblebee fastened to an enormous crazy quilt of a thousand colored remnants:

"Buy some potatoes."

"Buy corn."

"Buy Indian corn."

"Buy some barley meal."

"Over here, pes, housewife."

"Here it is."

"Take a look at the cabbages."

"Look at my stewed corn."

"Have a look at my ground corn."

"Come and see my potato tortillas."

"Hi, friend! Where have you been keeping yourself?"

"I've been feeling mighty low, comadre."

"Mighty low."

"Housewife. Have a taste of this."

"It's very good."

"It's very tasty."

"That's enough."

"Come here, pes."

"Just come here a minute."

"I'll throw in a little extra with your purchase."

"Make it three little extras."

"Just come over here."

"Housewife . . ."

"Let her see."

"Let her try it."

"Let her buy it."

"It's pretty expensive."

"It's cheap."

"What do you want, pes? Nothing is being given away."

"Nothing."

"Given away?"

"Dying to get it."

"Dying to have it."

"Housewife . . ."

"I want a good bit extra with a purchase."

"Just the usual extra amount."

The cries of offers and demands became entangled

above a surging wave of heads, hats, ponchos, shawls, coarse woolen worn by little babies, and coarse cotton awnings. From time to time a donkey's bray, a child's weeping, a beggar's curse would rise up to clash with that cloud of mingled sounds.

From the church balustrade the gentleman engineer, a young man with tanned skin, large hands, leather jacket, and military boots, Don Alfonso Pereira, with a country work suit: black leggings, riding pants, a whip in his right hand, a straw hat, the gentleman priest, the Ruata brothers, and Jacinto Quintana and the three policemen under him who stood a little behind the others were all spying on the multitude at the fair, savoring the exquisite pleasure of the skilled hunter confronted by the most highly prized game. They spoke of anything just to kill time, but every now and then they would exchange ideas about their plan:

"When the right time comes, we'll have to station ourselves at the four corners of the plaza so that not a single person can escape us."

"Not a soul."

"That's the way to do it, pes."

"Over five hundred Indians will come now according to what Policarpio told me."

"Just for this?"

"Just for this."

"More will go with us. Many more."

"Certainly."

"Everyone I have won over from the pulpit."

"Every single, one, pes."

"And those whom I tell to go."

"Oo-oo-ooo . . ."

About noon, according to the plan already agreed upon by that military staff who spent more than an hour and a half discussing it on the church balustrade, the policemen, mayordomos, sheriff, priest, the members of the Ruata brothers' patriotic group, Don Alfonso, and the honorable engineer swung into action.

"This way!" shouted one of the Ruata brothers, opening a path for the crowd to follow, and, with two policemen working with him, blocked one of the corners. Jacinto Quintana, the honorable priest, and Don Alfonso did the same at the other corners.

When they saw the plaza bottled up by such illustrious personages, nobody refused to go to such a patriotic and Christian labor. Quite the reverse, there was enthusiasm and joy. Refusal would have been an unheard-of crime. Nevertheless, the women were distrustful; they slipped away. But after taking a wooden cup of corn liquor or a glass of pure brandy—the first gifts of Don Alfonso Pereira—the people flowed through the town's main street in a parade of ingenuous chatter and small heroic prides. At the head of the great serpent which was being organized went the school children, followed by the children without schooling: ragged, gaunt, swollen-bellied urchins trying to hide their anemia and ignorance with a distressed smile.

Then came a group of septuagenarians carrying patriotic banners and sporting tricolored ribbons on their soiled straw hats. Logically, that sentimental head of the parade—the children and old people—saturated with tenderness, ingenuousness, austerity, sacrifice, with a grimace of strange joy, with the martial chatter of innocent victims, produced an emotion, a shiver of winged disquietude, in the cholas who were watching the spectacle from a porch or a doorway in tight little groups. One of them at this moment blew her nose on the inside of her skirt, and that noise was enough to set all of them off in hysterical, uncontrollable sobs that issued from their lips between small hiccups as of pleasure and pride. That edifying example swayed all those who watched. Everyone joined the parade.

"See how right I was?" the priest said to the owner of Cuchitambo as the success of the venture became evident.

"Yes. You were right," grudgingly conceded Don Alfonso Pereira as the warmth of an imprudent gratitude spread glowingly over his breast. His strong-man role ought not to be softened by such foolishness.

"Our people possess fine human qualities," said the engineer with great sincerity.

"Qualities which we must be careful to use to our advantage. Feelings with which we could put a stop to the many disorders, revolutions, and crimes which plague the world."

"In that you're right."

"It's quite evident. I am a genius at plucking the heartstrings of others whenever I put my mind to it," the priest said with pride.

"Your occupation helps some. The practice . . ." joked the landowner who had succeeded in calming himself.

"An occupation which my friends occasionally make use of."

"Thank you."

When the throng reached the point where the town's main street ended and from where the short cuts and paths radiated to many different places, the elder Ruata brother, taking advantage of a halt in the procession that was milling around without knowing where to go, planting himself on a high point of land, shouted as loud as he could:

"All of us! We, all by ourselves, are going to realize the fondest wish of our lives: the road. No . . . We don't have to ask favors of anybody. Do you hear me?

Just with our own hands and our own hearts we'll do all this. And of course . . . with the help of our good teacher . . . Of our good teachers: the good priest and dear Don Alfonsito of Cuchitambo. They . . . They will later become the great men in our Ecuadorian history . . . They because they have pointed out to us that we should do these good things . . . They'll be as great as Audón Calderón, as Bolívar, pes."

The crowd, reacting to the spellbinding oratory of the elder Ruata, raised their flags, their tools, their sticks, their palms, and their fervent voices to heaven:

"Bravooo!"

"Vivaaa!"

Such great success made the orator cry out, raising himself up on tiptoe:

"Like Bolívar who will be sitting at the right hand of the Almighty Father!"

"Bravooo! Fine lad!" howled the mob in a delirious effervescence.

And again the fists, flags, picks, shovels, arms, and voices rose and fell—and more than once.

The elder Ruata then proudly thought: "When I go with my younger brother to Quito, I'll just bowl over the intellectuals there with these phrases of mine."

"*Vivaaa!*"

"With this business I've won the confidence of Señor Alfonsito. And he's such a great man. I hope he'll get me a good job in Quito . . . And my brother, too . . ."

After the throng crossed narrow paths, scaled fences, climbed zigzag trails, and the pennants had been torn by the brambles and cactus, their enthusiasm covered with dust, their hope laden with fatigue, they finally arrived at the edge of the great mountain pass. From this vantage point they captured a view of the Indians scattered over the countryside like a string of ants. They were the Indians from the huasipungos of Cuchitambo who, since they hadn't needed to be convinced, had been marched to the work area at dawn. The throng commented with its hundred voices:

"That's the place, pes."

"They are right there."

"Look at the Indians."

"We must get to the foot of the hill."

"Over there."

"Run, pes."

"The Indians are good men."

"They arrived ahead of us."

"They sure did."

"Right over there."

"It's far from the town and close to the hacienda."

And, in truth, the work got underway, according to the orders of the military staff, more than two kilometers from Tomachi and only a few hundred meters from the manor house at Cuchitambo.

In a torrent of creaking carts, hoarse shouts, and clouds of dust, the mob, panting with enthusiasm, raced down the slope, and when they arrived alongside the Indians, each one, with faith and devotion, took his place in the great labor which everyone hoped would bring bread and progress to the area.

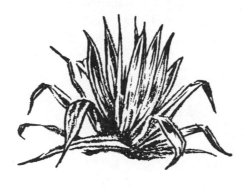

O N THE FIRST, second, third, and even the sixth night the majority of the workers returned to their village or their huts to sleep. But by the second week, since the journey home was becoming longer and longer, many of them remained and slept under the skies. And when night fell, the cholos from Tomachi and neighboring places in the region, in groups determined by their divers mutual interests—friendship, fellow-paisanos, kinship, love, food, or some plan for the future—gathered around small bonfires which the women kindled and stirred to drive away the freezing winds of the mountain peaks. Then the cholo men and women sought the shelter of a ditch, of a hollow in the rock, of a tree, or of a thicket, on top of which they would put any kind of clothing which they used both as umbrella and overcoat. The Indians on the other hand, enveloped in two or three ponchos, remained immobile as ageless stone alongside the embers of the bonfires. But by the third week, like a contagious virus which announces its disease by symptoms of fatigue and cursing, many were murmuring in a low voice:

"When the hell will this come to an end?"

"When the hell, cholito?"

"Our homes are abandoned."

"Our babies with their grandmothers."

"I thought that pretty soon . . ."

"Pretty soon."

"Don't even think about it."

"Oo-oo-oo . . ."

"What'll become of my crop?"

"Who'll look after my little chickens?"

"They're with the girl, pes."

"And who'll look after her?"

"We left everything willingly."

"Just for the pure novelty of it."

"The men maybe you're right about, pes. But the women . . ."

"Because they're so man-crazy."

"It was all because of the priest."

"Because of Don Alfonso."

"For Jacinto."

"For the Ruata brothers."

"Always putting the blame on others. Each one of us was wrong."

"Wrong."

"And now the provisions we had are all gone."

"I'll give you a little of mine. My boy went to the village and brought me enough for three days."

"That's good, pes."

"Because with the chicha and the chili stew that the bosses supply us our bellies are not filled."

"A poor man's belly."

"Food is always necessary."

"Some serve with their money and some with their person."

"That's really, pes, what patriotism means."

"Yes, that's it."

"Ave María. I don't understand it."

"It's hard to understand these things."

"It's for people who like fads."

"And for the man-crazy girls."

"And coming here with the babe in arms."

"Pes, there wasn't anyone to leave him with."

"And I was stupid enough to come here with my new clothes the first few days. They're a mess now."

"Well, it seemed like a fiesta."

"Fiesta for being screwed!"

And these complaints created a climate with a heavy, bilious, and unsuitable atmosphere. The mocking and happy chatter at night around the bonfires—dirty jokes, stories of ghosts and souls in agony—dwindled away to an expectant silence, into a kind of stupor of oblivion. Like circular retables of faces poorly lighted by the fire and strung on the thread of their mutually-shared anxieties, the workers looked askance at one another or, stupified, searched for a good omen in the caprice of the flames; or they scratched their toes with big cactus spines to ease the itching of the chiggers, or dozed curled up under their ponchos.

As for the women, those who had babies to nurse suckled them without blushing; those who were unattached slyly lay in ambush for the young peasant boys, and those who had husbands or lovers slept alongside of them. Since the personages of the military staff of the roadwork and those of the patriotic junta spent their days giving orders and their nights beneath tents, gambling at cards, guzzling brandy, and making love to the single chola girls, they didn't fall prey either to fatigue or to boredom. Nor could the Indians give themselves that luxury. They knew in their heart's blood, with a kind of sullen resignation, that the patrón, the priest, and the sheriff ruled their destiny and that, at the end of it all, their entire work and sacrifice would remain in the hands of those three. Nevertheless there were restless and devilish nights. Once the fires were out, in the mystery of the darkness when all were snoring in their refuges—holes in the slope, a bed of dead leaves under chilca and bramble bush leaves, a shelter in a dry ditch, a hut of rags—strange shadows glided amorously about. There were kisses, sweet complaints, heavy breathing, libidinous sounds, on the grass, under the thickets, beneath the cart that had arrived from the village, very close and appetizing for the few who could not sleep and who thought with mixed envy and reproach: "These God-forsaken wretches are screwing. I wonder who they can be. Maybe it's my . . ." But all of this was extremely far away for those whose fatigue was melting away in a deep slumber.

And that night, old Melchor Alulema from the nearby village in the hot jungle area of Cutuso, huddled up and sleepless because of malarial fever, heard, filled with suspicion, this slobbering mutter of the devil. He had heard it at other times, but his accursed chills, which put him flat on his back and filled him with bitter indifference, immobilized him. No . . . He couldn't go out looking for his wife and daughter who were missing from his side. Moreover, he never could distinguish females by their plaintive sounds of pleasure; a sigh as of agony made them all sisters under the skin. And he shouted despairingly:

"Rosaaa! Doloritaaas!"

"Shut up, goddamit!"

"At least let us get some sleep."

"Complaining old man!"

"The old bastard!"

"That's the way women are . . ."

"Man-crazy . . ."

"They live it up away from their masters."

Always the same chorus of voices, cruel and mocking, rising up from the ground. And Melchor still insisting:

"Rosaaa! Doloritaaas! Answer me, goddamit! Where have you gone off to? Speak up so I'll know you aren't the ones who . . ."

"Shut up, goddamit!"

"At least let us get some sleep!"

"Complaining old man!"

"The old bastard!"

"Doloritaas! She . . . Well . . . But the child, a virgin . . ."

One night the discontent of the cholos was aggravated. It was nature, blind, implacable. It must have been very late, one or two in the morning. The darkness, a thick drowsiness, seemed to snore lulled by the monotonous music of the crickets and toads. Suddenly, over the black platform of heaven rolled a clap of thunder with a cavernous rumble. Startled and worried, the people, now fully awake, clung to one slim hope: "No . . . It's nothing . . . It'll probably pass by . . . When it thunders a lot it can't rain very much . . ." But the volleys from above continued, stronger and deafening. This proof of the coming storm obliged the workers to seek new places of refuge.

The tents were soon filled by the more daring chola girls. Luckily, neither Don Alfonso Pereira nor the priest were there that night. The Indians, too, sniffing in the darkness in an instinctive search for shelter, went scurrying in all directions. But unfortunately, the only places even half secure had already been occupied by the cholos.

"There's no room for those dirty Indians."

"Nooo."

"Just get out of here, goddamit!"

"We're all filled up here."

"Filled up."

"This place is only for whites and cholos."

"Their lice."

"Their stench."

"Out, goddamit!"

Gusts of wind, icy, cutting, wheeling about over the camp of the mingueros—a hillside at a perilous incline—scattered the first shower of thick drops.

"We're in for it, cholitos."

"Now for sure."

"It's raining, goddamit."

"Not a single place for shelter."

"It had to happen."

"Such uncertainty in the sky."

"Such a distance from the village."

"We've done plenty."

"Plenty."

"Come. Come quickly."

"Where are you, pes? I can't see you."

"Over here."

"The mud."

"The water, mama Nati."

"The heavy shower, mama Lola."

"What shall we do, pes, mama Miche?"

"Just bear it."

"Bear it, goddamit."

"Daddy! Taiticooo!"

"If we only had some rosemary and holy wood to burn. It works so that the Almighty Father would save us from the lightning."

"From the lightning."

"And from the rain, who'll save us?"

"Nobody, pes."

"We're really screwed."

"We're screwed."

"You won't seek shelter under the trees."

"It's dangerous."

The Indians also mouthed, as though they were chewing roast corn, curses, prayers, and oaths:

"Taiticuuu."

"Boniticuuu."

"Mommy."

"Darling."

"Are we going to die at the hands of the evil mountain spirit?"

"Are we going to die, pes, at the hands of the evil wind spirit?"

"You good-for-nothing Indian."

"You Indian sinner."

"You stupid Indian."

"Goddam!"

With the first drops of rain, the air began to smell of moist earth, fresh cow dung, rotting wood, and of wet dogs.

"Will it pass us by?"

"Won't it?"

"I wonder what's going to happen, too."

But the fury of the storm obliterated all the human voices with a single roar. Like mute, blind shadows the Indians clung to each other in a childlike desire to banish the loneliness and fear from their hearts and heads. It rained with a seemingly tireless fury, and, in only thirty or forty minutes, which was a whole century to the drenched mingueros, the lashing water flooded the earth, filtering through the gorges of the hill, through the cracks in the rocks, through the winding ravines, and over the jutting edges of the boulders, mingling its boiling clamor—running, prancing, overflowing—with the shouts and laments that once again could be heard across the length and breadth of the camp:

"It's still . . ."

"A fierce downpour."

"Fierce."

"It's worse, pes."

"It's not letting up."

"I feel soaked to the skin. Just look at it now."

"God must have forgotten us."

"Cover yourself with this sack."

"Ooh-ooh-ooh. Everything's a mess."

"The mud, goddamit."

"We've really been unlucky."

"And what now?"

"The water's running over our feet."

"How about over there a little?"

"It's just as bad."

"How about over this way?"

"It's just the same."

"We're really screwed."

"Just have to wait till it passes."

"Just have to wait."

"Our clothes are dripping wet."

"My head."

"My back."

"Come closer so we can keep warm."

"The warmth of the human body."

"It's just the same as before."

"Nothing left to do, pes."

"Goddam!"

Nevertheless, the cholo men and women, clinging to their battered shelters—a hollow, a plank, an improvised hut, an opening between boulders and rocks—once more stirred with a desire to live.

From time to time, revealed by a stroke of lightning, one could make out the Indians who had remained under the inclement skies without shelter, groping their way through the mud in the downpour, immersed in the water that filled every corner and ruined every Indian hut and poured down every slope.

In a few minutes the rain again became more intense. Once more it punished the blind, mute earth, numb with cold. Overwhelmed by that tragic insistence at times monotonous, at times heavy, the workers choked off their comments, their prayers, and their oaths.

IN THE SAME LAZY, sad way that the dawn draped itself over the mountains, the workers aroused themselves. A whitish mist of voluptuous shapes, they crept along the surface of the soaked earth and began their childish chatter: the complaining gossip of the cholas, the curses and oaths of the impotent masculinity of the men, the shivering of the malaria victims, the coughing of the tuberculars, the weeping of the little babies for the mothers' breasts.

Slowly, from behind some thickets whose leaves had been torn off by the storm, a few Indians appeared, dripping mud, fearful and suspicious as worms surprised by the light, for whom the clumsy movements of their bodies and even life itself were a surprise after a night in which they thought they would die. Ten, twenty, a whole troop lifted their heads out of the mud, stretched their limbs with the painful sloth of numbed joints, shook out their dripping garments, their ponchos, their work shirts, their denim pants, and seemed to repeat mentally in a prayerful fashion: "It's over, taiticu . . . It's over, mommy . . . May God reward you . . ." And when they could see their muddy hands, when they could wipe their shirt-sleeves across their noses which were dripping mucus, and when they could speak, their lament was timid and in an imprecise murmur:

"Brrrr. Achachay."

The dawning hours void of sun (the sun so necessary to dry out the damp cold of the numbed flesh, the weeping eyes, the purpled skin, the uncontrollable chattering of teeth, the respiration made difficult by the altitude sickness) increased the murmur:

"Brrrr."

The wind off the paramo, icy and insistent, whirling with a biting embrace that glued the damp clothes to the stiff bodies, whistled in the workers' ears:

"Brrrr."

Without daring to take any action other than for their work, with their heads fallen on their chests, the workers exchanged sidelong glances and murmured:

"Brrr."

Something stronger than the desire to flee, something in their vitals that conquered the tragic obstacles, something that they had acquired through the ages—perhaps their accustomed way of reacting, an impulse implanted in their ancestors by the taita Inca, the pride of patriotic manliness of the cholos—kept the villagers and the Indians united and firm in their arduous collective task.

But before the work began and before the sun began to heat the day, there suddenly occurred a loathsome spectacle which demanded urgent attention. One of the

Indians, right after hastily arising from the mud under the thickets, leaned on a tree and started to vomit, writhing and moaning. The workers near him commented:

"Good God! What can it be, pes?"

"The altitude sickness."

"Ave María."

"And what now?"

"Poor Indian."

"They should give him a little salt."

"Sugar is better."

"Give him some cactus liquor."

"A glass of brandy."

"Brandy passes just like water."

"And where can we find such things, pes?"

"Yes, where?"

The spectators gathered round the sick man and formed a compassionate, trembling circle of insistent advice:

"We should take him down to the valley."

"That's the only way."

"And who'll take him, pes?"

"Make him roll down the slope."

"He'll get to the hollow in a single roll."

"To the hollow, goddamit."

"You, Lauro María. Pick up the Indian by his other arm," one of the cholos said to the worker who was on his right moving forward to help the sick man.

"Me?" asked the man spoken to.

"Who else, then?"

"Goddam!"

At the very moment that the two prudent cholos picked up the Indian, feeble and in convulsions, One-Eyed Rodríguez, who was an important worker belonging to the patriotic junta of the Ruata brothers, appeared and asked:

"What are you doing, pes? Why are you carrying him?"

"Just down to the valley."

"He's sick."

"He has altitude sickness."

"Where are you from?" the one-eyed foreman asked the sick man.

"I'm from where the patrún Alfonsu Pereira lives, pes," muttered the Indian in a faint voice.

"Ooh. Then you'll just have to leave him. The patrón has ordered that no damned Indian can leave here."

"But it looks like he's croaking, pes."

"Croaking? That's crap! I'll just cure him right now," said Rodríguez, giving himself an air of importance.

"Cure him of altitude sickness?"

"Certainly. Here is the whip which is daddy and mommy for all Indian ailments," answered the one-eyed cholo, exhibiting with sadistic pride the lash that dangled from his hand.

"It looks like a bull-whip."

"It's for a stubborn mule."

"It'd be better to just take off his poncho and tie him to the same tree where he vomited his guts out."

"Oh? Sí?"

"Sí."

"O.K., pes."

When all was ready and to the taste of the one-eyed man, the Indian half naked and tied to the trunk, the whip hissed like a snake several times over the sick man, who cried out:

"Taiticuuu."

"Let's see if there's a soroche that can resist this treatment, goddamit!"

"Taiticuuu."

"Take this, and this."

"Ouch! Ayayay! Pes, no more. It's O.K. now."

"Let's see," said the cholo Rodríguez, and he stopped the whipping. Then examined the victim.

"Enough . . . Enough, taiticu . . ."

"You're sweating now, goddamit. You feel better?"

"Yes, arí, taiticu."

"Ahah! You see now . . . ," concluded the one-eyed foreman addressing the workers who were observing the cure.

"It worked just as he said."

"I fixed up the Indian. He's not the first one, either. Higher up on the slope, where I spent the night, I restored the health of three young Indians who had been sorely attacked by the soroche. What a soroche, sonofabitch! Well then. To obtain the best result from the warming I dealt out to the Indian it would be advisable to give him a double shot of brandy."

"Of course, pes."

"Just get the brandy."

"The kind they call God's own drink."

"Up to now . . . It's not as screwed up as I thought . . . Only one Indian this morning was stiff in death, huddled up like a bird," said One-Eyed Rodríguez.

Filled with morbid curiosity, the workers ran to the small ravine indicated by the cholo. In the bottom, among some bushes, half-buried in the mud, they saw the cadaver of an Indian that still kept intact the attitude of his death: the legs drawn up front, the hands clenched against the belly, a strange smile on the lips that revealed tartar-incrusted yellowed teeth.

"Look, pes, the poor wretch."

"I wonder where he's from."

"I think he's from Guamaní. Judging by his black poncho, by his long hair . . ."

"By his fibre sandals, too."

"I wonder what his name is."

"Why—uh . . ."

"I wonder if he has any relatives."

"Poor Indian."

"If his relatives don't claim him it would be clever to make use of his being in the hollow and just throw earth on top of him."

"When the Indian sees blood he becomes a coward."

"That's so, pes."

"Who's going to find out about the poor wretch?"

"Yes, who?"

Near midday, Don Alfonso and the priest arrived at the minga. On learning what had happened, the friar and the landowner sought the best way of avoiding, by any means whatsoever, the weakening of that gigantic collective effort:

"It's impossible," Pereira insisted for the fourth or fifth time as he paraded his despair before the small tent belonging to the patriotic junta of the Ruata brothers, quite battered by the storm.

"Everything will turn out for the best. It's necessary to convince the cholos," said the priest.

"Oh, that . . . The Indians have borne the brunt of it."

"If one of these villagers dies we'll be cooked. We must thank the Lord that it was only the Indians who got screwed," said the priest.

"But the truth is that the workers are tired. They have no satisfaction, no coaxing to make them stay. We must not forget that everything they do and will do is voluntary, for nothing. Absolutely free," put in the engineer.

"Free," the landowner repeated worriedly.

"Well . . . In that case we're all of us in the same boat," said the friar with an extraordinary cynicism.

"And we mustn't forget that thanks to that force, to that impulse of tradition which these peoples still maintain, something will be accomplished."

"A failure at this time would be shameful for us. Everyone knows . . . They all know that we . . . I . . . ," said Don Alfonso Pereira, brusquely halting his pacing back and forth.

"An inducement. Find a satisfaction for the materialistic side, for the sinful flesh, for the insatiable belly. Oh, if it were only something spiritual! Well . . . I could . . . ," said the priest, his brow contracted with the strained gesture of one who is seeking the perfect solution to the problem.

"And we can't forget either that in two or three days we'll begin the hardest and most dangerous part of the work—the draining of the swamp."

"Most dangerous?"

"Hardest?"

"Sí, my dear friends. Two kilometers. That can't be done without hard work. That can't be improvised," the technical expert said. A mocking, vengeful impulse, for having endured the previous night's storm without his cronies, made the engineer put these obstacles and funereal perspectives before Pereira and the cassocked one.

"What would society say of us?"

"And Christian culture?"

"And our Fatherland?"

"And history?"

"And the business firms and the big shots interested in the affair?" said the engineer sarcastically.

"An inducement. You said an inducement. Sí. That's it!" exclaimed the owner of Cuchitambo. No . . . There was no other way. He would have to embark on a sea of expenses. Many expenses. His apparent generosity must not falter. His . . . "Accursed expense, goddamit," he thought angrily as he swallowed with a triumphant expression the bitter plan to which he had to accede.

"What is it?"

"Something . . ."

"Something definitive," cried the landowner.

"Aha!"

"Then . . ."

"More corn liquor and more chili and pepper stew. I'll give them brandy. I'll give them guarapo."

"That's great!"

"That sure changes the problem."

"Besides, every week I'll dish out a ration of corn and potatoes. What . . . What else can they want? Me . . . I'll pay for it all, what the hell!"

"Magnificent!"

"Terrific!"

"A man like this . . ."

"Are you satisfied now, mister engineer?"

"Well . . . we'll see . . ."

The Ruata brothers, Jacinto Quintana, and One-Eyed Rodríguez sprinkled this piece of news among the workers, exaggerating a little, of course. That very evening barrels of brandy and fermented cane juice came in from the town.

The business was handled by the sheriff's wife. With the money that Don Alfonso had advanced her she dispatched without delay two muleteers and five mules on a trip up-country to look for brandy and brown sugar. As for the guarapo for the Indians, she threw into some huge clay jugs which she had kept, forgotten, in a backyard shed bucketfuls of water, unrefined sugar, wine, rotten meat, and her husband's old shoes to speed the fermentation of the brew.

B Y THE TIME the work had progressed to the swamp the minga had recovered its enthusiasm and fortitude. Of course, the panorama which now confronted the workers was not very promising. It held a gloomy, quiet vegetation of cattails, watercress, and dwarf grass. There were strange, mocking noises emerging at certain intervals only to fade into a faint echo on the horizon. And at dawn the treacherous mist enveloped everything in long strips, which the sun would later dissolve. A suffocating sun covered with a sweaty steam and skeleton clouds of mosquitoes.

From the very beginning, the workers commented with a provincial pride on the imposing and lethal aspects of that region—"the best in the world." But the telegraph operator, an occasional worker when he wasn't busy with the usual breaks in the line, who as a young man had made trips into the Amazon jungles, said mockingly and with obvious scorn:

"Crap. This is just a small quagmire. In the East there are really horrible swamps. In those I saw when I was a young man there was no way to get in just like this, pes. They're very deep and they're crawling with crabs or whatever the devil they are, so that when any beast or human falls in, in less than five or ten minutes the flesh is eaten away to the bone. That is a real swamp. This one . . . It's just a baby swamp."

"And what about the tadpoles, millions of them?" put in one of the troop of cholo workers who usually stayed on the edge of the swamp looking with superstitious fear on that surface filled with tumors and deep holes covered with wet matted grass.

"As if they can hurt you."

"But, goddamit. It's dangerous to go in."

"Sí, pes."

"If we must remove our shoes or sandals and leave them on the edge of the swamp, anybody can just take them away."

"And lift your pants legs above the knee."

"Working in water all day long."

"Not that, goddamit."

"It'll just be for the Indians who are already used to such labor."

"After all, we're half-white."

"How will it be done, pes?"

And of course, it was the Indians who, fit for any risk, ventured, planted up to their thighs, among the cattails, among the watercress, or in the open swamp, to comply with the engineer's orders; the cholos were busy elsewhere.

At times, staying three or four hours in the cold muddy water would give an Indian cramps, but the miracle-working brandy soon liquidated his difficulties. Jacinto Quintana and his wife, whom Don Alfonso Pereira had made responsible for the distribution of the corn liquor, the fermented cane juice, the alcohol and the pepper stew, spent all day and all night taking care of the workers. They even slept under a shed, in a structure improvised from sticks and straw from the paramo. And when an Indian came by, asking for the corn liquor or the fermented cane juice, and was reeling more than was required for the therapeutic dosage needed to insure the maximum work yield, the sheriff, anticipating the Indian's request, would shriek:

"No, goddamit! First get to work. When it's necessary we ourselves . . ."

"We ourselves will call you, pes taitico . . . ," the chola Juana would say consolingly.

If the one who arrived in such condition was a neighbor from Tomachi the sheriff would then joke:

"You're feeling no pain now pes, cholito. It would be a good idea for you to sweat it out by working a little to cure your hangover."

"Cure me? I am cured."

"The hangover, I mean."

"Aaaah!"

If the worker became stubborn and silly, Juana, shrewd and coquettish, would take over:

"O.K. . . . I'll give you a little glass of a brandy that I have."

"That's fine. Just what I'd like, goddamit."

"Provided you come with me and join in the work with the others, pes."

"With you, my cute neighbor, anywhere."

"Shall we go?"

"Let's . . ."

When for any reason whatever the sheriff and his wife noted that a worker would go for several hours without taking any alcohol, they immediately and anxiously sought, by flattery, jokes, or daring caresses, to dose suitably this rare personage, who was in their eyes a potential deserter.

During those days, especially among the Indians, the malaria became acute. The sick ones huddled up alongside the shed of Juana and Jacinto in a retable of small bundles trembling beneath their ponchos, their eyes ablaze with fever, their lips dry, poisoned with fatigue and lassitude, and their voices feeble:

"Water. Bring me water."

"Brrr."

"Taiticu."

"My darling."

"Brrr."

"Goddam."

When the number of malaria victims became a goodly one, One-Eyed Rodríguez, who always bragged about his infallibility as a healer, entered the game. After downing a glass of brandy with Jacinto Quintana he proudly declared:

"This prescription I learned in Guallabamba. Over there the malaria is a dangerous thing. Even becomes pernicious, pes. The Indians at the charcoal furnace area I also cured like this."

One-Eye ordered his assistant, a small and silent young Indian:

"Go, Tomás, and fetch me the lamb hides. The peeled hides which I had brought in from the village. The ropes and the jug with the medicine, too."

"Yes—arí, taiticu."

A few minutes later when all was ready, Rodríguez and the small and silent young Indian helped the malaria victims to their feet and covered their backs with the hides—a parchmentlike, hairless armor—which the one-eyed man had brought. Then he had them form a circle, one behind the other, telling them to bear as much as they could and to run as though playing a children's game. And then the skillful healer took his post in the center of that wheel that gyrated slowly with its old ponchos, its trembling bodies, and its bent heads. Rodríguez, angered by the slowness of the suffering Indians, cried out, raising the whip which hung from his right hand:

"You'll have to run until you sweat."

"Ay!"

"Run, goddamit! Run!"

The threat was not sufficient. As they jumped and stumbled around, they soon were rendered helpless by the malarial fever.

"You call that running, pes? If I don't use the whip you'll take the easy way out and we'll be stuck here until tomorrow. Now you'll see! Now goddamit! Here's how . . . !" screamed the one-eyed man to the rhythm of the whip, which alternately stretched and shrank with hissing explosions.

"Ouch! Ay!"

"Run, goddamit, run!"

The fear of the lash which, as it embraced the slowest man, sounded like a knife tearing through the parchmentlike hides, increased the speed of that human wheel to a painful vertigo.

"Ouch! Ay!"

"Run, goddamit, run!"

Fatigued to a point of exhaustion, the runners began to fall to the ground. But the man with the whip, enchanted by the enchantment of ephemeral power, by the music of the lash on the dried lamb hides sometimes, and on bare Indian legs or faces others, or occasionally through the air itself, redoubled the force of his blows.

"Ouch! Ay!"

"Run, goddamit, run!"

At the end, the three or four Indians still on their feet completed their last circle almost on all fours, and, bathed in sweat, lurched to the ground with weird shiverings. It was impossible to demand more of them. Disjointedly, with an agonizing rasping in their breathing, their lips parched with fear and fever, they looked at the healer with imploring glassy eyes, a troubled and diabolical entreaty which seemed to be camouflaging something very like a criminal threat.

"You sweated! You really sweated, goddamit! I drained your filthiness, you dirty Indians!" exclaimed One-Eyed Rodríguez, cocking his head to favor his good eye so he could better observe his handiwork. Then with a proud cry, he called his assistant:

"Tomás, go and bring me the jug of medicine and a wooden cup so I can finish with these slobs!"

Each victim had to swallow a good ration of the beverage prepared by the one-eyed man: brandy, the juice of bitter herbs, a small dose of urine from a pregnant woman, a few drops of lemon juice, and ground guinea pig excrement.

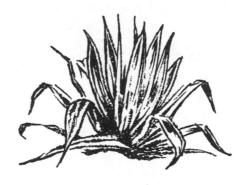

THE SLOWNESS with which the road was being pushed through the marsh and the dejection which had spread through the cholos—at that point the majority of them disorderly, the others enduring unwillingly under the weight of small personal inducements—caused Don Alfonso to say to the engineer:

"We've got to finish this in two or three weeks."

"That's quite easy."

"But . . ."

"Patience above all, Don Alfonso."

"Patience!"

"The terrain forces us to go at a child's pace, very slowly. It makes us feel our way . . ."

"Oh, you've gotten it into your head that the ditches have to be started from the mountain. And that, my dear friend, takes a lot of work . . ."

"I can't see any other way."

"Don't you?"

"That's what the plan calls for."

"And what about a parallel ditch cut some twenty or thirty meters from the planned road? A drainage ditch that can be finished in a few days?"

"Oh! That . . . Put the workers in the swamp, bury them in some hole or other . . ."

"And what do you think I've bought the Indians for?" asked the landowner with a cynicism steeped in age-old custom.

"Oh! O.K. If you care to drain the swamp with Indian corpses."

"I didn't say that."

"Then what?"

"We'd save some 50 per cent in time and labor."

"I'm not saying it's impossible . . ."

Don Alfonso Pereira exhausted all his bold arguments. In truth, he wasn't interested in the Indians as such. Not at all. What bothered him greatly was the urgency to complete the road and the need to fulfil his pledged word. Ten or twenty young Indians really weren't very much to his estate of household goods, chattels, livestock . . . That was why he had paid plenty of money for the Indians. "Every effort for the country's

welfare demands sacrifice, bravery, audacity . . .
Maybe in war also we don't lose soldiers . . . ," he said
to himself, attempting to justify the criminal cynicism of
his arguments to his conscience. At last the engineer
murmured:

"Provided you are ready to lose a few peons."

"Nothing's going to happen, my dear friend."

"Better you should believe that."

"In case something bad happens for any reason at
all I'll have them bring the leather lassos from the
hacienda."

"The leather thongs?"

"Of course. In a moment of danger we would easily
save the person sinking by tossing him the lasso so he can
keep from going down."

"We won't help anyone that way. If the swamp
doesn't get him he'd die being yanked out with the lasso."

"We'll make the rescuers wade out very close to the
victim."

"Anyway you look at it he'll be a dead duck."

"Oh?"

"From such a hole no one could pull him out."

"My ropers could."

"Well, then . . ."

On the next day, to Don Alfonso's pleasure and delight, the work on the ditch began. Led by two experts in
such matters, Andrés Chiliquinga and an Indian from
Guamaní, a troop of Indians entered the swamp.

"Be careful! Begin the ditch a hundred meters from
here!" shouted the engineer standing on the edge of the
swamp. With him were the priest scattering benedictions,
Don Alfonso, Jacinto Quintana, almost all the members of
the Ruata brothers' patriotic junta, and some cholo workers of both sexes. The engineer watched how the troop of
Indians, sinking above their ankles, advanced into the
marsh and how they labored to remove the mud-laden

plants and the muck itself, from their feet.

But the afternoon of that very day, just a few minutes before the time to quit, a voice from some cattails over one hundred meters from the edge cried for help. The cry created a pause laden with suspicion and fear in everyone's mind. Indians, cholos, and gentlemen quit their tasks and strained to hear.

"Taiticuuus . . . !"

"Over that way!" someone said pointing to the right, into the very heart of the swamp.

"Of course, over there!"

"Oo-oo-oo . . ."

"You can see him clearly in the cattails."

"Just the upper half of his body."

"Only a half . . ."

"How could he have wandered so far away, pes?"

"Yes, how . . . ?"

"Stupid Indian."

"And now what?"

"Goddamit!"

"Wait . . ."

A hundred and fifty meters away, more or less, hidden at times by the shadowy twilight and by shreds of mist that were lazily creeping across the drenched earth, the silhouette of an Indian, cut off at the waist, raised its arms in tragic desperation.

Amid the surprise of some, and the useless efforts of others, the engineer approached Don Alfonso Pereira and in a haughty mocking voice said to him:

"You see now I was right. He's the first Indian to fall into some hole. He won't be the last."

"Oh, what damn stupidity! Now you'll see how we take care of this," answered the landowner, really worried. And going over to the Quinteros' shed he called for his rescuers:

"Caiza, Topanta, Quishpe!"

"Patroncituuu."

"Come here."

"We're already preparing."

"Come, and bring the thongs!"

As though by magic, three Indians appeared before the patrón, ready to play their part—without ponchos, their denim trousers rolled up to the thighs, carrying long leather straps in one hand and the lasso in the other.

"You'll have to save a bastard who got himself stuck in the mud," said Pereira.

"Arí, su mercé. But Chiliquinga—who knows how— has to come with us, pes."

"So take him along."

In spite of the intoxication that lent strength, resignation, and hope to the cholos of the minga, the outcries of the victim unleashed a host of comments:

"That's what we were spared from, goddamit."

"This is really dangerous."

"No one can tell where he will lose his hide."

"And his hide is the only thing a poor man owns."

"The only thing they don't take away from him just like that."

"The only thing."

"Goddamit."

"What will the priest say now?"

"What he always says. Punishment from Taita Dios."

"Punishment."

"I only hope it won't rain in the night."

"I only hope they don't get a hold of me to drink with Jacinto."

"I only hope they can pull the Indian out."

"Yes, save him."

"If he disappears it won't be good."

"No, pes."

"Oo-oo-ooh . . ."

"Holy Mary."

"Mama."

"I won't . . ."

All this time the silhouette of the young Indian trapped in the hole kept shouting and desperately waving its arms. The rescuers cautiously entered the swamp, guided by Chiliquinga, who felt his way along with every step so painstakingly that the workers on the edge of the swamp lost their patience:

"Quick! Hurry, pes!"

"How, goddamit? First I've gotta feel my way along to see if the muddy grass is safe, if it'll hold the weight of the Indian or of a cholo. Here, first . . ." Then a little later, "Here, pes . . . Now then I can advance the other foot . . . My big toe tells me just when it's mud to step on, and when it's water to avoid. Uuuy . . . Thinking such stupid things, I just now almost slipped," Chiliquinga said to himself while the onlookers were shouting.

"Quick! Hurry up, goddamit!" Don Alfonso commanded.

"Ave María . . . Taiticu, su mercé, also wants me to . . . There is no way, pes, to go any faster. My lame foot isn't gripping firmly, it doesn't sustain me . . . ," the expert Indian responded mentally.

"Hurry uup!"

By this time the victim was buried up to the chest. His arms flailed more hopelessly, and his cries slowly became fainter. He now seemed a trembling blur amid the fog and the cattails.

"Quickly! Hurry up, goddamit!"

Andrés Chiliquinga raised his hand in a signal to show it was impossible for him to penetrate further and very carefully retreated a few steps as he cautioned the rescuers:

"Right here . . . From this place . . . Ahead it's really dangerous, pes."

About fifteen meters from the trapped Indian the ropes inscribed flourishes in the air with long and ambitious strokes. A fearful and prayerful anxiety gripped the hearts of the mingueros who were watching from the swamp's edge.

"Mommy."

"Holy Virgin."

"Miraculous Virgin."

"How can it hurt you, pes?"

"Poor Indian."

"A miracle."

"Now! Nowww!"

This last exclamation, as though in triumph, merely meant that two of the three lassos thrown had encircled the victim, one by the waist, the other by the neck and one arm.

"Nowww!"

"Pull! Pull him out quick!"

"Before the Indian disappears!"

"Sí, before . . ."

"He's already disappearing, goddamit!"

"Pull!"

"Pullll!"

"Hurry!"

"What's the matter? They're not pulling."

"Now!"

Unable to find the sufficiently firm footing that the rescue of the victim required, the ropers and Andrés Chiliquinga came out of the swamp by way of the drainage ditch.

"What happened, goddamit? You're leaving the Indian to be swallowed up by the swamp," shrieked Don Alfonso.

"Patroncitu, taitiquitu. There wasn't any way to do it, pes. Our feet were just slipping on the loose, muddy plants."

"The damned mud. Alright. Let's see if from here . . ."

"From here certainly, pes."

"Then pull!"

The Indians pulled hard and spiritedly on the two ropes that the muck had imprisoned. On the two ropes that refused to move. Every effort seemed in vain. But the cholo workers thought it was their duty to help and they pulled also, burning the flesh of their hands on the black and dirty ropes. Soon the struggle became frantic between the people who were trying to save the victim— by that time submerged to his hair—and the strangling muck that held the Indian with greedy cruelty. At the end there remained, like a macabre trophy, only a disjointed puppet, the bundle of a cadaver covered with an old poncho.

"He's no longer breathing, pes."

"The rope around his neck."

"The wet rope can cut like a knife."

"On his waist."

"On his arm."

"It's too bad."

"Dead."

"I don't think he has any relatives."

"Nobody to protest."

"Nobody to weep."

With such comments the workers dissembled the secret fear and bitter rage which the rescue scene had engendered in them.

"It would have been better to have left him buried in the swamp," said the engineer.

"Who knows?" retorted Don Alfonso, frowning.

That night, taking advantage of the shadows and the sorrow that weighed on all of them, the first cholo workers deserted. Four days later the tragedy was repeated. Another Indian died. After a week only ten cholos remained on the minga: those of the Ruata brothers' patriotic junta, the sheriff, and his wife. And even the engineer one morning let it be known that he wanted to quit.

"We must not aggravate our problem. The honorable Minister would be very happy to know that you . . . Well . . . That you are spoiling our plans," Don Alfonso Pereira said with venomous slyness.

"Our plans?"

"Certainly. To ruin everything through childish sentimentality. The government must show that it does enterprising things, that it helps individual initiative."

"I . . ."

"Nonsense, my dear friend. Great accomplishments require great sacrifices. And if we study the case painstakingly . . . Right now the sacrifice is mine."

"What do you mean?"

"The Indians who are dying and who will die, let's say five, ten, twenty, are mine . . . I am losing capital to develop publicity that you and the ministry can then make use of where you work," said the landowner.

"That's so. But . . ."

"There are no buts about it. More are killed in war and nevertheless no one mentions it."

"No one," muttered the engineer in a voice and attitude of complicity, of defeat.

"I say this to you in confidence. You shouldn't worry much about my business affairs. The Indians cost me very little. I can't remember if they were five or ten sucres apiece."

"Five or . . ."

"Sí. I have no reason to lie to you. And on the other hand the road is the future of this whole region."

In spite of the priest's giving masses in the field on the edge of the swamp, alongside the clay pitchers of fermented cane juice and the barrels of brandy at the shed of the sheriff's wife, and offering the mingueros great discounts in the sufferings of purgatory and hell, the cholos did not return to the work. It was the Indians, and only the Indians who, in eight weeks of violent threats and orders by the patrón (who seemed an enraged demon), in eight weeks of the almost daily macabre spectacle of inexperienced Indians falling into the holes and having to be rescued, in reality conquered the swamp, draining it and stretching a wide road across it.

Once the dangerous, tragic stage was passed and the work was once again on solid earth, on mountain slope and valley pastures, the Ruata brothers' patriotic junta entreated the population of the towns of that region—cholo men and women—to join in a second minga to complete the work. That appeal was not in vain, and the half-white people again contributed their disinterested efforts. Besides, in addition to the chicha, the guarapo, the brandy, and the peppery chili stew, Don Alfonso presented extraordinary cock fights (a passion of the rural people) which filled all conversations and banished all anxieties.

"They're going to fight out on the plain, pes?"

"Right out on the plain."

"Then I'll have to bring my mottled cock who is a real devil."

"Oo-oo . . . You'll steal their money with that, pes."

"And my red one?"

"He's no good any more."

"What do you mean, pes? He's become a fury."

"I also have one."

"The fights are going to be very good ones."

"Very good."

"I won't miss them, goddamit."

"Hurry up and finish the work soon."

"Real soon."

"They say that the workers from Callopamba are coming with the cock that won the championship there."

"Is that so?"

"That's what they say."

"Then patrón Alfonso's cocks haven't a chance, pes."

"Not a chance."

"What do you mean . . . ?"

"Hurry so you can see them."

"Hurry so you can get ready."

"Four or five fights in each match."

"My money."

"You just wait and see."

"Well, it's something new."

"It's something stupid."

Only the Indians stayed on the job after four in the afternoon. The cholos, pompous and restless, gathered together in every nook, forming circles that ringed the consecutive cock fights. The most important fights, between the champion cocks of the area—Don Alfonso's, the good priest's, those belonging to certain arrogant villagers—took place next to the new shed of Juana and Jacinto. This was an improvised structure of old sticks and green straw on the far side of the marsh, faithfully advancing with the minga. The bewildering, hypnotic shouting then went on until night and prevented the workers from even thinking of anything else.

"We have to get them evenly matched."

"They are evenly matched!"

"I'll bet three against six."

"Double?"

"Of course!"

"If I had the money, I'd take you up so you'd learn not to prattle so."

"I'll pay, goddamit!"

"He was screwed."

"That's just how it is."

"The bastard's got guts."

"Guts."

"How can that be?"

"Yes, how?"

"Don Teófilo's black cock is here."

"My buddy's one-eyed one."

"Abelardo's mottled one."

"The one-eyed one!"

"The mottled one!"

"Now you'll see."

"Raise your claws, you bastard!"

"Raise them!"

"Aaay!"

"He got him in the neck."

"In the eyes."

"He can't go on any longer."

"Lower your beak."

"He's not falling."

"He's tricky."

"How clever! A ringer."

"He didn't seem like one."

"Goddamit."

"He's a real killer."

"A fine rooster, pes."

"In two attacks."

"In two spurrings."

"I can't believe it. My five sucres."

"I lost three."

"Ave María."

"I'll get even on this other one."

"I'll offer double."

"I'll pay double."

"On which one?"

"It's too late, pes."

"The other is a good one."

"The other one!"

"Bravoooo!"

"He's got him screwed!"

"Your mother, you mean."

"Yours."

"How?"

"Face to face! Face to face!"

"Síííí!"

"Suck his head."

"To remove the blood."

"The comb."

"Give him some brandy."

"Clean off his beak."

"It'd be a miracle."

"A miracle."

"The judge . . ."

In the shadow of that anesthetizing entertainment enhanced by the guarapo and the brandy, nobody was concerned about the landslide on the hill where three Indians and a boy were killed. And so the minga came to an end. And so the road that later became the pride of that region was constructed.

Publicity many times had brought Don Alfonso both satisfaction and annoyance. But he had never imagined that the sleepless nights and the expenses he had to face on the minga—everything done for his own personal interests—would crown him with the reputation of a patriot, of an entrepreneur with immaculate virtue. The press of the entire country decorated their pages with praises and photographs which extolled the heroic feat of the landowner, the engineer, the parish priest, the sheriff, One-Eyed Rodríguez, the Ruata brothers, and the cholo workers. And what about the Indians? What had become of the Indians all at once? They had mysteriously disappeared. Not a single one to be found anywhere, in any report. Well . . . Perhaps their appearance, their quality didn't fit in with the publicity. Or maybe they hadn't been present at the time the pictures were taken.

"How excellent. How excellent, goddamit!" Don Alfonso muttered when he finished reading the latest article sent him by his uncle Julio. Toward the end it said:

The future of our country, seeking a sure way to develop resources which till now have remained unexploited in the Eastern jungles and its subtropical areas like that of Tomachi, has taken a decisive step forward. From what we know at present it seems that the colonizing nations are looking for, and rightly so, appropriate areas to establish themselves. Regions with good roads, favorable climate, proximity to urban centers, large areas of workable land of good quality, etc. etc. If we believe that the settlers, simply because they are foreigners, will just come and immediately penetrate the heart of the jungle, deprived completely of all human aid, and work miracles, we will be seriously mistaken. We must promote foreign investment by providing everything it needs in its areas of investment. That is what is demanded of us for the investment of the foreign capital of the world's great nations. In the case we mention, the civilized nations will now have a wide field of action before them. Some one has asserted that the case of the colonizing nations and Don Alfonso's patriotic deed can be compared to the opium traffic in China. This is vile slander, we claim. We who have always stood for justice, for democracy, and for freedom.

TANCREDO GUALACOTO—whose huasipungo was on the river bank, and who had the reputation of being rich because of the fine flannel ponchos he wore to Sunday mass, because of his well-stocked henhouse, his cow and calf, and his guinea pigs—had been selected sponsor for the final fiesta which the town was offering as thanks to the Virgin of the Spoon for the successful conclusion of the community road-building labor.

That morning, Tancredo Gualacoto followed by a few companions, José Tixi, Melchor Cabascango, Leonardo Taco, and Andrés Chiliquinga, stepped into the porch of Jacinto Quintana's house where the chola Juana was selling guarapo to the Indians.

"Let's have a few cents' worth of the aged stuff, pes, mama señora," requested the future *prioste*, seating himself on the earthen floor with his friends.

Mechanically, without answering, a few minutes later the chola put down alongside of her clients a blackened wooden vessel filled with a yellowish liquid on top of which was sailing a cup fashioned from half a gourd. With the cup Tancredo generously divided the drink fairly among his companions. He then seized the vessel in both hands and in one final swig drank up what was left of the beverage. He immediately ordered another four cents' worth. He had to stoke himself with courage, had to make himself strong, in order to seek out the priest and ask for a little reduction in the fee for the mass. It had been impossible for him to raise all the money he needed. They had given him seventy sucres for the cow and the chickens, which was not enough to cover the church expenses. The advance which he asked of the hacienda was for the vespers, for the brandy, and for the band of musicians.

When they had drunk up the third wooden vessel of guarapo, Tancredo Gualacoto and his friends felt brave enough to confront the priest, to ask him, to demand of him. The interview took place in the courtyard of the church where the holy father was accustomed to walking back and forth after his lunch—to insure a good digestion.

With primitive terror, sneakingly, as one approaches a wild beast to hunt it down or to be devoured by it, the little band of huasipungueros approached the priest:

"Ave María, taiticu."

"Forever praised be her name . . . What do you wish?"

"Taiticu."

Gualacoto, with hat in hand and head lowered, stepped out from the group, and, after a pause laden with doubt and anxiety which caused him to twist his head like an idiot, muttered:

"Taiticu. Su mercé. Boniticu . . ."

"Speak up. Tell me. God is listening to you!"

Before the name of the almighty Father the future prioste felt his heart leap into his throat. But nevertheless he muttered:

"Can't you just come down a little, su mercé?"

"Eh?"

"Just a little on the price of the mass."

"On the holy mass?"

"It's high, pes. And I'm so poor. Taiticu, boniticu. Where can I get it from? Pay you, su mercé, buy guarapo, chiguaguas—fireworks, chamiza—firewood . . . For my little cow and chickens I could get only seventy sucres."

"Well, you can ask the patrón for an advance."

"Not a chance, pes. The little he gave me isn't even enough for the guarapo."

"You're a rich Indian. Everyone knows that."

"Me—rich? What do you mean, pes?"

"Then you'll have to look somewhere else."

"Ooh . . ." Gualacoto and his friends murmured with a disillusion and despair that annoyed the priest a little.

"How can you imagine, and the rest of you, too, stupid accomplices, that in an affair so important, of such religious significance, the Virgin will be pleased with a cheap ordinary mass? No! Not at all! Impossible!"

"But . . . I don't have, pes . . ."

"Taiticuuu," begged the chorus.

"You wretch! And you'd better not haggle any more, for the Virgin will be angry. And once she is angry she could easily punish you from above."

"Ave María!"

"Boniticu."

"That's enough, I don't want to hear any more."

The reaction of the tasteless guarapo on the Indian's meekness then fermented into bilious bubbles, fiery hands, and a longing to cry out. Gualacoto insisted, his voice now a little insolent:

"I don't have it, pes!"

"But for drink you've got it, you corrupted Indian."

"What's wrong with that, pes?"

"But when you should venerate the Holy Virgin you act foolish. For a measly hundred sucres you have fallen into sin. God is witness to your stinginess. He's watching us now . . . When you die He will really collect all you owe Him."

"No, taiticu."

"Yes, of course He will!"

"But . . ."

"No buts about it. You'll go straight to Hell. To the biggest caldron of all."

"Taiticu!"

"No doubt about it. You're doomed."

Feeling more and more trapped, doomed, with the priest's threats ringing in his ears, the future prioste reacted by slipping into the first stages of an insolent drunkenness:

"So what's that to me, damn it."

"Eh? What did you say, you Indian animal?" shrieked the priest, his hands twitching in the audacious Indian's face, with a horrified gesture that sought to prevent any possible reply. But Gualacoto, almost instinctively, insisted:

"Damn it."

Quickly, and with a histrionic versatility, the priest realized that it would be better to assume a beatific expression. Then he raised his hands and his glance toward heaven and, with the faith of a character out of the Bible, began to question—in a friendly, confidential chat—imaginary persons in the sky, a giant canvas of grey dropsical clouds:

"Dios mío! My blessed Virgin! Merciful saints! Restrain your wrath. Withhold your curses from these poor wretches."

"Taiticuuu," the friends of the reprobate implored in a chorus.

"No, Lord. Don't rain your fire on this unhappy Indian, on this accursed Indian, on this Indian animal who has dared to doubt you, to doubt your most holy Mother, to doubt me. No! It isn't fair to hurt and punish an entire village simply because of the idiocy and wickedness of one of its sons. The worst . . ."

As an opportune assist to the priest's tragicomic monologue, with the timeliness with which chance sometimes surprises us, a peal of thunder rolled across the heavens. It must have been raining up in the mountains. Panic then seized the future prioste and the chorus of Indians that accompanied him. The Almighty Father had answered with a cavernous voice and a lash of lightning. Oh! That conquered all anger, crushed all rebellion. Tancredo Gualacoto and his accomplices melted away with a sinuous cunning.

"Lord! I understand your anger is just–and holy. But . . . withhold your angry arm from punishing them. Blasphemy . . . ," continued the pious priest and as he lowered his glance to look at the sinning Indians he saw that they had all disappeared.

"Indian idiots!"

Glutted with terror–with the unreasoning fear of those who feel themselves pursued by supernatural forces –the accurst Indians, after moving through the village like silent swift shadows, reached a short cut that twined up the hillside. Maybe they were seeking their huasi-pungo, or a ravine, or a cave that would shelter them. But Taita Dios . . . Taita Dios is implacable . . . As they ran, and as fatigue made their pulses race and their lungs choke for breath, their fear became overwhelming, and strange, threatening voices pursued them:

"Scoundrels! Heaven-cursed creatures! Enemies of Taita Dios! And of his Virgin mother!"

"Noooo."

"Aaaay."

Each fugitive tried to exonerate himself in a low

voice, tried to evade the punishment, the eternal damnation:

"No, Taiticu."

"That miserable Gualacoto was to blame."

"That wretch."

"I just happened to be along."

"How can I be blamed?"

"I'll even give a hundred-sucre mass, and one of two hundred sucres also."

"It's Gualacoto. It's entirely his fault, pes, Taiticu."

"Pardon us."

"Taiticuuu—Lord."

"It's all his fault."

"The scoundrel. The wretch . . ."

That tormenting emotion, a mixture of revenge and fear, which had surged uncontrollably over Gualacoto's friends melted into sighs as they saw before them their familiar huts on the banks of the river. They were their refuge against all evils. In them awaited their babies, their women. There they lived together amicably with indifference and scorn for the possessions of earth and of heaven. There . . . Ah! Feeling themselves safe, though they were panting like beasts, the Indians halted a moment to look up the valley. Instinctively, they sought their reconciliation . . . But, suddenly, with a hoarse clamor that rolled along down the river, the countryside awoke and the air shuddered, laden with the smell of moist earth. Yes, a hellish din roared down from the horizon.

"Accursed!"

Once more Gualacoto and his companions felt panic. Threateningly red, swollen with mud-laden waves, the river raced through the mouth of the big ravine and painted both banks with scenes of terror and desolation.

"La creciente," muttered one of the Indians of the

group surrounding the future prioste.

Then from every corner of the valley echoed the same words, multiplied a hundredfold:

"La crecienteeee!"

From the hovels huddled along the lowland there poured forth clamoring women, old Indians stumbling with anxious impotence, children swift as frightened birds, and infants inexpert in their flight. They issued forth in a terrified race—with a terror that explodes blindly, aimlessly, abandoning everything they owned: the crops, the animals, the bed on the floor, the clay stewpot, the cooking stove, the tattered clothes, and the goatskins. And that chaotic clamor mingling with the slavering fury of nature saturated the whole scene with tragedy.

"La crecienteee!"

"Ooooh!"

Occasionally, when the confused clamor lessened a little—without any fresh prey for its maw—one could hear the cries of some Indian woman who had forgotten a tiny baby in the straw bed, or a tied-up dog, a cow with its calf, her chickens, her guinea pigs, or her paralyzed grandfather.

"Ayayay! My baby, gone forever!"

"Ayayay! My poor papa, gone forever!"

"Ayayay! My poor little dog, gone forever!"

"Ayayay! My little corn field, gone forever!"

"Ayayay! My little guinea pigs, gone forever!"

"Ayayay! My clothes, gone forever!"

"Ayayay! My beloved!"

Meanwhile, impassively, the crest roared on its way, inundating everything, rolling along spilling tragedy with each violent pulse of its waves. It continued to spray the banks of the river with an almost human contempt, with the remnants of things and of lives that it had sucked into its maw in its mad race through the valley. On the brown backs of the raging waves one could discern on a macabre voyage: the gate of some corral, an uprooted tree, a pig, a tree trunk, a rag, the body of a child. When these passed by, some of the Indians stationed on the river's high banks would, with a sort of naïve daring, toss their leather lassos out over the whirling waters.

"Mommy."

"Little angel."

"Wonder whose baby that is."

"Me, too. Whose can it be?"

"Could be José's?"

"Or Manuel's?"

"It looks like an Indian baby."

"So whose can it be?"

"And whose little pig is that. It looks like a black pumpkin."

"It looks like the Alulemas' pig."

"No, theirs is a red one."

"Ave María."

"It looks like one of the hacienda cattle."

"Jesus! It's a white man."

"Or an Indian more likely."

"An old man."

"A young man."

"Maybe it's a child."

"It seems bigger."

"Almighty Father. Why this, pes?"

"Use the lassos."

"The lassos!"

"Ooooh!"

Weary with looking, with commenting, with toiling uselessly, the groups of Indian men and young women on both banks sank into a silence of stupefying pain. Suddenly someone suggested:

"Let's see what's down below."

"Where, pes?"

"Where the river widens on the plain below."

"Aaah!"

"Good idea."

"Sure is."

"Let's go, goddamit."

"Let's go."

Eager for some scrap of news, even if it was bad news, the Indian community scrambled downhill. The uncertainty of their first movements very soon exploded into a mad flight. Everyone had lost someone or something: a son, a grandfather, a wife, a dog, a very close friend, the remains of the huasipungo. In their dizzy scramble toward a goal not at all secure—falling and stumbling—with fatigue thumping in their lungs, the Indians ran, as though they were hypnotized, across corn fields, jumping ruts and ditches and hurdling the bramble bushes. They would have killed or let themselves be killed if someone had dared to stop them. The detours and roundabout course they were forced to follow increased their anguish. What did it matter if they sank to their knees in the mud, if they were scratched by the brambles and the spines of the cactus, if they slid on their rumps down the rocky slopes, or if they waded up to their thighs in the backwaters?

When the multitude arrived at the small valley where the river lost its banks and spread over the field like a sheet, everyone went into the water sorting out the flotsam—a refuse of rags, straw, sticks, mud-laden plants and small ropes—of the huasipungos swallowed up by the current. Then they stopped, crying loudly, alongside the macabre discovery of the cadaver of a child, of an old man, or of some animal.

"Mommy!"

"Dear one!"

"My beloved!"

"Who will I live with, pes?"

"Who will I work with, pes?"

"Ayayay, Almighty father!"

"There's a corpse of a white man and a dead animal."

"With a cadaver from a hut and huasipungo."

"Ayayay, Taiticu."

Then each of the bereaved retrieved his beloved corpse and all he could of his huasipungo.

Meanwhile, the Indians who had gone with Gualacoto, once more paralyzed and crazed by that feeling of guilt which the priest had sown in their souls, hadn't allowed themselves to be trapped by the folly of the crowd. They stood motionless, saturated with despair, with hatred, with revenge, and looked about them for someone to attack.

"Goddam!" exclaimed one of them, his eyes roving about—searching for something, for someone . . .

"Why, pes, goddamit?" muttered another in the same way.

"Why, pes, Taita Dios?"

"How are the babies to blame?"

"How are the women to blame?"

"How are the animals to blame?"

"How are the crops to blame?"

"How is the hut to blame?"

"Goddamit!"

Trembling with anger, not knowing where their rage could lead them, José Tixi, Melchor Cabascango, Leonardo Taco, and Andrés Chiliquinga stared at Gualacoto with deep suspicion. And in each of their breasts awoke a demon of perverse revenge with an insidious voice crying "Accursed ones! The punishment of Taita Dios is . . . ! Because of you! The holy priest . . . !"

"Goddamit."

"Taiticu."

"Noooo."

Blinded with superstitious terror, the friends of the future prioste mentally sought to excuse themselves inwardly: "It was his fault . . . For being stingy with the Virgin Mother . . . Papa priest said . . . He said . . ."

"It's that Indian . . . the animal . . ." exclaimed Tixi, facing the accursed one defiantly.

"He was stingy with Taita Dios and the Virgin Mother!" echoed the others approvingly in a voice completely devoid of self-control and of compassion.

"Me? How come, pes?" asked Gualacoto retreating with a panic that made his eyes bulge wildly and his dark cheeks turn pale.

"That's what the boss priest said."

"That's what he said."

"You're to blame—just you."

"No, taiticus."

"Yes—arí!"

"Arí, goddamit."

Gualacoto's marked fear and humble words added fuel to the burning and confused desire for revenge of his friends. The ponchos fluttered, and they raised their fists like clubs.

"Me . . . I'm not to bla-a-ame . . . ,"

"You miser . . . Arí, goddamit," the chorus replied, savagely venting their anger.

Feeling he was lost, Gualacoto fell on his knees, begging for pardon, for mercy. No one listened to the words and prayers of that accursed being, for there was within them an inner voice that maddened the Indians of the chorus to the point of driving them to crime: "We are damned because of him. Stingy with the Virgin Mother! The punishment . . . The flood . . . Death . . ." And so it came about that in the excitement of a nameless cruelty the pleas of the victim—Gualacoto stretched out on the ground—were converted into moans and these moans were at the same time transformed into agonizing, painful gasps.

"Take this, goddamit."

"Take this, you miser."

"Take this, you damned Indian."

And when they tired of the punishment the Indian Taco announced, noting the quietness of the fallen man:

"I really believe he's a dead duck."

"Dead duck?"

"Arí, pes."

It was at the sight of the blood that stained the earth and the poncho and face of the victim and of the club which one of them had plied without pity that Gualacoto's friends and executioners fled in disorder.

Since the tragedy of the flood was a greater one, and since every one was bewailing his own sorrow, the disappearance of the Indian reputed to be rich only bothered his relatives.

"He was swept away by the flood," one of them said.

"By the red devil," said another.

"But why, pes?"

"For being so miserly with the Virgin Mother."

"Eh?"

"That's what the taita cura said."

And that was the truth. The saintly priest, taking advantage of the intoxication of panic and terror that left the Indians almost hypnotized, proclaimed that punishment to be a warning from heaven against the stinginess of the faithful in their alms, in the payment of the responsories, the masses, the holidays and the mourning.

"Punishment from the Lord! Pun-n-n-ishment!"

"When he says so, it must be so, pes," the Indians

and cholos thought to themselves, and, inwardly intimidated by that fear, they knelt at the priest's feet, gave their money freely, and humbly kissed his hands or cassock.

The church holidays, the masses, and the responsories yielded the priest sufficient funds to buy himself a truck to transport cargo and a bus for passengers.

"I won't leave a trace of a beast of burden," the priest would exclaim each time his drivers would hand him the profits from his new business venture. And, in truth, he wasn't exaggerating. Little by little, the horses, mules, and burros were left with nothing to do and earned nothing. And so a goodly number of mule-drivers who had worked through the length and breadth of that region became unemployed and spent their days with their grief and nostalgic memories. On the other hand, in the country, especially on Don Alfonso Pereira's hacienda things changed in the opposite way. The patrón had ordered more fields sown than usual; and mother nature was being generous. That year, at the sight of the ripened crops the peons muttered:

"This year yes, pes. The patroncitu will reap plenty."

"Plenty."

"He's going to give a good amount this year to the poor Indian."

"Who has nothing at all because of the flood."

"Ave María. Because of the flood."

"Who has no corn."

"No potatoes."

"Nothing at all, pes."

"Like a homeless cur."

"Like a pebble in the road."

"Dying of want."

"Of starvation, too."

During the cutting of the barley, when the mayordomo heard these laments he muttered in a brandy-soaked voice (he had already sampled much of the guarapo that the patrón had ordered for the peons):

"That's all you think about. Finish quickly, goddamit."

"Oooh . . . Ha ha ha . . ." responded the chorus of Indian men and women, half-hidden by the waving spikes, before they bent again over the earth with that slowness that bites into kidneys already mouldering with fatigue.

"Hurry . . . Hurry so I can give you a good shot of guarapo."

"God will reward you, taiticu."

"Ooooh . . ."

In the afternoon, riding a big mule, ill-humored and nervous (and bursting with greed for the good business he was able to transact on the new road), Don Alfonso approached the edge of the field being harvested and in a rough voice called to the mayordomo, who was dozing off the hangover of a pleasant inebriation sitting on a guarapo barrel:

"Eeeh! Goddamit! That's a great way to manage the Indians."

"Patrón . . . I . . ."

"Look at him. Doesn't even know what's going on. You were sleeping, weren't you?"

"Just at this moment, su mercé."

"Will the guarapo last for the whole harvest?"

"There are quite a few workers here, patrón."

"And who has drunk up almost the whole barrel?" Don Alfonso asked in a threatening voice.

"You see, su mercé. It's like this . . ." muttered the cholo, approaching the fence where the patrón was, so that the Indians wouldn't be able to hear his lying excuses.

"Who?"

"The work is very hard. I've given them twice already."

"You must make do with this. I'm not going to spend a penny more on it."

"We'll get along O.K., patrón."

As Don Alfonso began to leave, he turned suddenly toward the mayordomo, as though a very important problem had called him back, to exclaim:

"Ah, I've told you more than once. Now I'm insisting on it. If by chance some young Indian comes along for chugchi and offers to help so he can trick you out of the gleanings, you just kick him out. Is that understood?"

"Sí, patrón."

"I've ordered the same rule for the other fields, too. That barbaric custom is gone forever."

"Just what you say, pes."

"Let them buy. They'll have to pay me. That's why they're working . . . That's why they have money . . . Those who haven't borrowed from me yet we'll sell on discount."

"Ooooh . . . Every single one has used up more than his pay."

"Then they're damned well out of luck."

"Well . . . you see, patrón . . ." the cholo began to object, reminding the gentleman that it was a question of an old custom rooted in that somewhat partriarchal tendency of great landownership.

"What do they imagine, that I'm their daddy and mommy? What do they think? The chugchi! The chugchi! What they really come for is to steal from the crop and not just to pick up the left-overs."

"Don't speak so harshly, patrón. If the workers find out what you plan they'll just stop their work without finishing. Don't you see that they've always had that right?"

"Oh, yes? Good. Goddamit! We'll make them finish

the work even if we have to beat them. Aren't they *my* Indians?"

"Of course that's right," the mayordomo concluded with an insipid smile, as though only at that moment had he discovered that truth. It was his fear of the patrón's anger that . . .

"Several women who came from the village thinking I was going to be as stupid this year as in the past and give them the chugchi I really sent packing. Let them find some other man to take care of them."

At that moment, falsely interpreting Don Alfonso's haughty mimicry with the cholo, a few young Indians of both sexes left their work and came up to the fence. Quickly forestalling any inopportune request, the master, addressing the mayordomo, asked:

"Have they already had their guarapo? Did you give them plenty?"

"What I . . ."

"Even if Juana charged me all the money I had for the twenty barrels that I bought just for the harvesting, I want them to drink up, I want my Indians to be happy."

"Patroncitu."

"If they haven't drunk any, let them have some."

"May God reward you, taiticu," murmured the chorus of Indians, thus undoubtedly putting off for later or for some other occasion the request that they had wanted to make.

"That's exactly what we'll do, pes," the mayordomo said in a sly mocking tone.

"Just let them take another shot. It is always good to be kind. Just look at the poor Indians, sweating, tired . . ." Don Alfonso Pereira said as though he were scolding the cholo Policarpio, who, with his head lowered to hide the impudent smile of an accomplice, replied in a weak voice:

"That's right, patrón."

Satisfied with his cunning maneuver of feigned generosity the master dug his spurs into the mule and took the road to the village while the cholo mayordomo, his brain awhirl, understood as a direct threat the prohibition of the chugchi, the . . . "Ah! It was never like this. The patrón himself. He had never been so bad. The crops were never so good before. It's not fair, pes. The tragedy of the flood was all his fault, too. He told me not to clean out the river. He's the one. And so then? Goddamit! In good conscience he really should give them something. Something anyway. Oooh . . . But I . . . It's better that . . . He can screw me . . . Really screw me . . . Dirty Indians, miserable wretches, good-for-nothings . . . On the other hand, he . . ." the cholo was thinking as he turned mechanically to the barrel of guarapo.

"Drink up. Drink, you villainous Indians. You've got a good patrón to thank for this. A good patrón . . ." Policarpio exclaimed as he divided the beverage among them. It seemed necessary to him that they, that he, that everyone should believe what he asserted.

THE WIND striking the door of Andrés Chiliquinga's hut imprudently opened it to reveal its wretched, dirty, black, and sordid entrails. In the corner where the stove stood, the Indian Cunshi was roasting corn in a grimy clay potsherd. Since the corn had been stolen from a neighboring huasipungo, she, filled with surprise and defiance, greeted the intruding wind with a sullen face: brow furrowed, eyes weepy and stewing in the smoke, lips half-opened in a grimace of ill-defined anguish. When she realized what was happening she ordered the child:

"Go on, longu, fix the crossbar on the door. The neighbors will be spying on us."

Without answering, with face and hands smeared with black porridge, the little boy—he was four—got up from the dirt floor and obeyed the order putting a cross-bar, very heavy for him, across the door. Then he returned to his corner where the clay pot with a little food in the bottom awaited him. And before he went on eating his scanty daily ration he cast a pleading, coquettish glance toward the earthen pot where the grains of corn were gaily and fragrantly leaping about.

"This is just for your taiticu. You already had your porridge," warned the mother correctly interpreting the child's famished glance.

"Ooooh . . ."

"Just wait a little. Together we'll steal some from daddy. A little sample for baby, pes."

In spite of this hope, the boy stuck out his lower lip and, without further preamble, squatting on the floor, put the clay pot between his legs and finished his porridge.

After speaking to his neighbors on the slope of the big hill, where hunger and the necessities of life had become more and more urgent—in that area the families of the huasipungueros displaced from the banks of the river were clustered in caves or in improvised huts—the crippled Andrés Chiliquinga climbed down by the short cut. It should be added here that the Indians who had lost their huasipungos and all the peons of the hacienda, some bitterly and some with naïve illusions, were expecting the socorros—the annual help—that the administrator, the owner, or the tenant on the land had always been accustomed to sharing after the crops had been harvested. "Will it be on the patron saint's day? Will it take place on Sunday? Maybe for the feast of the Holy Mother? Perhaps on . . . ? When will it be, pes?" the Indians asked one another as the days kept going by.

In truth, the socorros—one and one-half bushels of corn or barley—with the huasipungo loaned to them and ten cents a day wages (money which the Indians never even got a whiff of because it went to pay for, with no possibility of amortization, the hereditary debt of all living huasipungueros for the advances on the saints' or Virgins' feast days of the taita cura for the sake of the dead huasipungueros) made up the annual payment that the landowner granted to each Indian family for its work. Someone from the valley or from the mountain asserted that the patrón must have forgotten the traditional custom, but the gossip that ran through the village was different: "No . . . He won't give any socorros this year.

The Indians have been screwed." "They're screwed . . ." "He's buying up grain to fill his granaries." "He's buying like crazy . . ." "He's buying so he can fix his own price later when . . ." "We'll be screwed also, cholitos" "He won't give a single grain to anyone. Nooo . . ."

When the waiting period could no longer be endured and hunger was an animal barking in their bellies, a goodly number of the Indians, old and young, on Don Alfonso's property swarmed up to the patio of the hacienda in a dark, noisy, and unrestrainable group. Since it was very early, and drizzling besides, each one sought some shelter in the corners until the patrón should awaken and decide he was ready to listen to them. After a long hour of waiting they again solicited the help of the cholo Policarpio, who was going in and out of the house constantly:

"Be kind to us, pes, master mayordomo. Socorritus . . . We have come to ask for socorritus."

"For socorritus."

"The master mayordomo already knows."

The cholo, become more sly and proud because of the Indians' entreaties, spread news of vague hopes:

"Now . . . the patrón is up now, goddamit."

"We only hope so, pes."

"He's drinking his coffee. Don't bother him now."

"Taitiquitu."

"He's angry . . . angry . . ."

"Ave María. God help us."

With a big frown and a whip in his right hand, Don Alfonso showed himself on the porch that faced the patio.

"What's the matter? What do you want?" he cried in a grating voice.

Suddenly the Indians, both men and women, with a magical briskness and in an apparently humble silence gathered at a prudent distance from the porch. In those first few seconds—as they urged one another forward with little pushes and elbowings—not one of them dared to compromise himself by stating their urgent case to the patrón. Impatiently, tapping his boots with the whip, Don Alfonso again shouted:

"What do you want? Are you going to stand there like a bunch of idiots?"

Somewhat unhappily, and with the attitude of a dog fawning on its master, the mayordomo, who also would profit by several bushels from the socorros, spoke up:

"Well, it's like this, patrón. They've come to request a little charity from your worship . . ."

"Eh?"

"A little charity, pes."

"More? More charity than I already give them, goddamit?" interrupted Don Alfonso icily hoping to eliminate once and for all the daring attitude of the Indians. He knew . . .

"The socorritos, pes! The poor Indian is dying of hunger. He has nothing. They've always given socorros, su mercé," dared to request in chorus the Indians who were of the group displaced from the banks of the river. And then as if someone had opened the floodgate of the physical needs of that sullen, dark mass, all suddenly found their tongues to tell of the hunger of their babies, the sickness of their old people, the increasing boldness of the Indian girls, the tragedy of the devastated huasipungos, of the endurable misery of past years, and of the unendurable misery of the present one. It quickly became a threatening clamor, chaotic and rebellious, in which diverse cries would rise and fall:

"Socorrus, taiticu!"

"We've always received them!"

"All-l-l-ways!"

"The baby, too . . ."

"The wife, too . . ."

"Socorrus, a little corn to roast."

"Socorrus, a little barley for porridge."

"Socorrus, a few potatoes for a fiesta."

"Socorruuus!"

Like surging waves the supplications rolled on to the hacienda porch enveloping the increasingly nervous patrón, increasingly bathed in that fetid bitterness of the peons' outcries. But Don Alfonso, shaking his head, was able to shout:

"That's enough, damn it, that's enough."

"Taiticu."

"I've told you over and over that I'm giving you nothing this year. Do you understand me? It's nothing but a barbaric custom!"

"What do you mean, patroncitu?"

"That's what I pay you for . . . That's why I give you the huasipungos . . ."

"We need the socorritus, too, pes."

"You're still complaining, goddamit? Get out of here! Get out!"

The complaints stopped at once, but the throng stayed on, motionless, pertrified, grim. Meanwhile some miserly calculations went through the landowner's mind: "I must not give in. Four or five tons just to give away to these barbarians. No! They can fetch a good price in Quito. It would bring enough to pay the priest for the use of his trucks. Enough to . . . If I give in to them I won't have enough to do business with the gringos. Oh, they've met their match in me. They'll learn I'm a real man!" Mechanically Pereira took a step, two steps forward until he came to the edge of the first stone step of the porch. Then he arched the flexible whip handle with both hands and, breaking the silence, shouted:

"You're still here? You didn't hear me, goddamit?"

Stolid as a wall, the Indian throng didn't budge. Confronted with such resistance Don Alfonso for a few long seconds didn't know what to say. Perhaps for an instant he felt beaten, swallowed up by what he believed to be an unheard-of rebellion. What could he do with them? What could he do with his pent-up rage? Almost crazed with wrath he went down the three stone steps and, approaching the nearest group, he grabbed a young Indian and shook him like a filthy rag, all the while uttering half-choked oaths. Finally the victim was rolling on the ground. The mayordomo, fearful of what might occur, for he could see how icy was the fury in the eyes of the Indians, helped the fallen Indian to his feet and reproached the crowd in a loud voice so that all of them could hear:

"Don't be so ill-mannered. You shouldn't get the poor patrón so angry. He'll die of rage. He'll just die. What'll happen to you then? Don't you understand or don't you have any hearts?"

Hearing the cholo's words Don Alfonso felt himself to be a martyr to his duty, to his obligation. In a voice hoarse with fatigue he managed to shout:

"These . . . These Indians are driving me to an early grave . . . Me . . . I'm the one to blame, goddamit . . . For having spoiled them as though they were my own children . . ."

"Poor patrón," said the mayordomo, and instinctively, in defense against any possible attack from the outraged Indians, mounted his mule.

The landowner, on the other hand, inspired by the example set by the priest, lifted his eyes and hands to heaven and, in a voice that demanded an infernal punishment for his cruel enemies, screeched:

"Oh, my God! My God! You who watch us from above . . . You who have often told me to be harsher with these Indian savages . . . Protect me now. Defend me! Don't you hear me? Send a punishment for a warning to them . . . Or a voice . . ."

Don Alfonso's attitude and his request stunned the Indian throng. It was dangerous for them when the priest or the patrón began a dialogue with Taita Dios. Yes, it was. It was something superior to the weak efforts of Indians caught in the trap of the huasipungo, to the feebleness of men dirty, meek, and forsaken. They forgot the socorros, forgot why they were there, forgot everything. A desire to flee overpowered them and, immediately, some covertly, others openly, they began to dissolve.

"Goddamit! Turn the dogs loose on them. The fierce dogs!" the mayordomo then shouted, his kindness and fears abruptly transformed, with a devilish cynicism, into the cries and actions of an executioner.

The angry dogs and the whips of the mayordomo and the Indian servants of the patrón's house angrier still, swept the patio clean in a few minutes. When Policarpio returned to the patrón he said to him with slavering deviousness:

"You'll see, su mercé. Just now when I was chasing the Indians I overheard them swearing to return in the night to take the socorros by hook or crook."

"What's that?"

"They're starving. They could even kill us."

"That they may be able to do with some fool coward, but not with me. Here I am the power and the law."

"You're right, of course, pes," murmured the cholo, just to be saying something.

"Go at once to the sheriff and tell him to send me the two peasants who are his deputies. Armed . . ."

"O.K. patrón."

"Oh, and tell him to telephone Quito and ask the

Police Inspector in my name to send us a squad to crush any possible criminal uprising among the Indians. Don't forget: in my name. He knows what to . . ."

"Sí, certainly, pes."

The mayordomo went off like a shot from a cannon, and Don Alfonso, feeling himself all alone—for the huasicamas were, after all, Indians and could betray him, the cook and the female servants were Indians and would not inform him—was stricken with a strange fear, an infantile, stupid fear. He ran to his room and took the pistol from his night table and, with terror-crazed violence, aimed at the door as he shouted:

"Now, goddamit! Come on, now, you filthy Indians."

When the echo of his threat was his only answer he became somewhat mollified. Nevertheless he advanced a few steps and looked suspiciously in all the corners. "Nobody's here . . . I'm just like a woman . . ." he said to himself, and he laid the pistol down. Then, exhausted from the nervous fright brought on by the impertinences of the Indians, he flung himself headlong on his bed like a betrayed woman. Of course, he didn't cry; but instead sadistically evoked macabre scenes which proved to him the savagery of the Indians. How did they kill Don Victor Lemus, the owner of Tumbamishqui? By making him walk on a gravel path after first flaying the skin of his hands and feet. And they disposed of Don Jorge Mendieta by tossing him into a caldron of boiling cane syrup at the sugar mill. And Don Ricardo Salas Jijón by abandoning him on the mountain in a pit dug to trap beasts. "All . . . All because of stupidity . . . Because one doesn't give them what they want . . . Because one gets their lands or water through some court action . . . Because the brazen young Indian girls have been violated at a tender age . . . Because . . . All little insignificant things . . . Stupid things . . ." Don Alfonso thought.

That night, the presence of the two armed peasants and Policarpio restored his peace of mind. Nevertheless, when he went to bed he said to himself: "These criminals will rebel one of these days. And when that happens we won't be able to choke it off as we did today . . . Today . . . Then I'll . . ." A charitable voice vibrated hopefully in the great señor of the region: "The hell with those who come after me; I'll be gone by then."

"Yes. To hell with them," Don Alfonso muttered in the darkness, with a smile of diabolic selfishness.

Meanwhile, out on the porch, enveloped in the mystery of the country night, the two armed guards talked of their daily needs and their present fears:

"What did you see?"

"Something's moving."

"That's just the shadows of the trees, stupid."

"I heard something over on that side."

"You're seeing and hearing things."

"I wonder how long they'll keep us here."

"Gee! . . . My wife's having a baby."

"Did you hear something else?"

"There's no one there."

"No one."

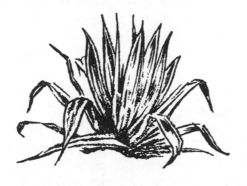

THAT YEAR was a dreadful one. Hunger, cunning and merciless, punished the people of the houses, of the huts, and those on the huasipungos. It wasn't the hunger of rebels who starve themselves to death for a cause. It was the hunger of slaves who let themselves be killed while savoring the bitterness of their impotence. It wasn't the hunger of the idle, out of work. It was the hunger that curses with exhausting work. It wasn't a hunger with the rosy, future prospects of a miser. It was a generous hunger which fattened the granaries of the highlands. Yes. A hunger which obstinately scraped a tune on the ribs of the children and dogs, a tune half complaint, half weeping. A hunger that sought relief in stealing, in begging, in prostitution. A hunger that every day exhibited large and small pictures of sordid colors and faces of a bilious, criminal pallor. A hunger of the gut, of the stomach, the heart, the throat, the saliva, the teeth, the tongue; hunger of the lips, the eyes, the fingers. Oh! A hunger which overflowed on the muddy paths of the mountains and down into the narrow streets of the town in the appearance of beggars' greedy hands, of children's wailing, of the cynical remarks of old Matilde, who that morning in the doorway of a hut was suckling an incredibly thin creature at her tired, dark, and withered breast; an infant who instead of voraciously sucking his nourishment was gasping faintly for air. The women who were passing by that scene commented:

"Why doesn't she give the baby some barley porridge?"

"Ooooo . . ."

"He's going to die."

"Seems that way."

"Even if it's only a little."

"There isn't any, pes, señora!"

"And goat's milk?"

"Even less."

"Something to replace a mother's empty breast, you good-for-nothing."

"We're all in the same fix, señora. Maybe you . . . ?"

"That's certainly true. If I had something . . . It hurts me just to see the little one . . . But I don't even have enough for my own babies."

"There's no corn, not a bit of barley, nor the help of the good neighbor who had his huasipungo on the bank of the river. Nothing at all."

"His appetite is uncontrollable."

"He doesn't want to take the nipple."

"Why should he? If only blood comes out."

"That's what comes out, señora."

"Uncontrollable appetite."

"Ooooh . . ."

"Encarnación's baby died the same way."

"Sí, pes."

"And Victoria's baby, too."

"It's like an epidemic."

But the epidemic of the children also struck the adults. The chola Teresa Guamán found her neighbor, a fellow from the coast whom they called Mono (the monkey), curled up on his bed just like a fetus, stiff, with a thread of bloody spittle drooling from his lips. The Indians commented:

"It's a punishment from the Almighty for having lived in sin with that woman."

"I believe the poor man was also a consumptive."

"It's a punishment . . ."

That same morning the cholo Policarpio came to the hacienda with an urgent matter for the patrón:

"We just went to round up the cattle . . . You see . . . Pes, we found, su mercé . . ."

"What? More complaints?" Pereira asked nervously. Ever since he had refused to give the socorros and was able to sense in the Indians' cunning attitude a vengeance that could block his plans, he could not fully rid himself of an unhealthy, ill-defined fear.

"The spotted ox is dead."

"The big one?"

"No, the old one."

"And how did it happen?"

"I don't know just how, pes. We found him stiff in a hollow on the hill. It must have been several days ago, because he's already stinking. He could have fallen off a cliff. Could be the epidemic . . . What else could it be?"

"So. What'll we do with him?"

"That's just it, patrón. But you see . . . I delayed a little because I was helping a few Indians remove the carcass from the ditch."

"And so . . ."

"And now the Indians want . . ."

"What?"

"Since the meat is already half rotten . . . They want you to give it to them, su mercé. I told them I'd ask you. Just ask you, that's all, patrón," said the mayordomo, on observing that Don Alfonso's face was wrinkled in a scowl of protest and amazement.

"That I should give them the meat?"

"That's what they say . . ."

"Give them the meat! I'm not crazy, goddamit. Now . . . right away you have a deep hole dug and bury the ox. Bury him deep. The Indians must never taste a single bite of meat. Goddam! Once they taste it they get to like it and then we're really screwed. Every day they'd make me slaughter an animal. They'd think up good reasons, of course they would. Give beef to the Indians . . . How stupid can you get! That's all we need. Not even a whiff of it, goddamit. You hear what I'm saying: not even a whiff. They're just like animals, they'd get used to the beef. And then who could stop them? We'd have to kill the Indians so they wouldn't kill off the cattle. For of two evil, tragic choices, we must always choose the lesser. So bury that carcass as deep as you can."

The mayordomo, who was being persuaded by Don Alfonso's clear and intelligent argument, wiped his flat, sweat-pearled nose on his poncho, trying to conceal a great cowardice, and muttered:

"That's how it'll be, patrón. I knew beforehand that you . . . But since they . . ."

"*I knew!*"

"Well . . ."

"Enough of that nonsense," shrieked the landowner. And then so as to sidetrack that affair which he now considered closed, he asked: "Haven't they spoken to you again about the socorros?"

"No, su mercé. But the dirty Indians are suffering. They must be plotting something."

"Something?"

"Sí, pes. Since they are just like animals."

"And what could it be?"

"I don't know, pes, patrón."

"Goddam! And so much fuss with the harvests. After thirty trips in the priest's truck there's not enough left even for seed in the granaries," Pereira complained, anxious to justify himself in this strange way.

"Sí, pes."

"Now what will they say? What will they try to do?"

"Nothing now, pes."

"So, all right. Hurry and get that ox buried. Hasn't a new bull come down from the mountain?"

"Just the one who killed Catota. The bull who killed him during the fiesta of the Virgin. The Indians who watch the cattle say they've seen him hovering once more close to the picket fence."

"How many head of cattle do you reckon we have now?"

"About six hundred, patrón."

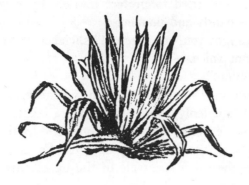

Following the patrón's instructions, the mayordomo, herding six Indians before him, took the path up the hill. The apathy which had characterized the Indians' work since they had been denied their socorros on this occasion seemed to give way to sprightliness, jokes, and laughter. In reality, the Indians who went with Policarpio weren't expecting the intoxication of guarapo, nor the gorging of their gut like a prioste, but they knew about the dead ox, and they were stirred by the hope of a smell of beef and of being able to steal a slice and take it to their huts under their ponchos.

One of the hacienda dogs who had followed the mayordomo, suddenly discovering the unmistakable scent of rotten meat, raced ahead with his nose high in the air. Instinctively, the Indians, jostling each other and laughing, hurried after the animal. The mayordomo easily guessing the peons' intention, spurred his mule, and, lifting his whip on high, shouted:

"Where are you running to, goddamit?"

No one paid attention to him. He had to put his hand on his lasso rolled up on one of the saddlebags. At the throwing of the lasso one of the Indians dropped to the ground. The fallen Indian, finding himself under the mule's hooves, tried to protect himself by covering his face with hands and poncho.

"I caught you, you wretch!" shrieked the cholo in a triumphant voice.

"Taiticu."

"And now the rest of you will see, goddamit."

But suddenly, on descending a zigzag path, a flight of some twenty buzzards, frightened by the dog and the noises of the Indians, rose into the air. Then all could see the sorry spectacle of the ox carcass. At once the comments rose like flies:

"Ave María."

"The Almighty's favorite food—just ruined!"

"A mess."

"The buzzards have just begun, that's all."

"There's plenty of meat."

"Plenty of entrails."

"Sure are."

"It smells rotten-ripe, ready for cooking."

"Forget that 'plenty' and that 'ready for cooking.' Get to work and dig a deep hole, you Indian loafers."

"A deep hole?"

"Sí, to bury the animal."

"Ave María!"

"Taiticu!"

"Bury it like a human being?"

"That's the patrón's order."

"Taita Dius is punishing us, pes."

"That's none of our business. It's white men's affairs."

"It's a punishment because it shouldn't be done this way."

"You're being punished because you become like beasts when you get a whiff of beef."

"But everyone's the same way . . ."

"Get busy digging that hole, goddamit."

As the Indians dragged the carcass over to the hole to bury it, a hole dug with unusual speed, each one succeeded in hiding a good-sized chunk of the fetid meat under his poncho. Andrés Chiliquinga also, who was one of the burial crew, did as the others did. The ox, with his entrails spilling out, his eye sockets empty, his rump torn open by the fierce beaks of the carnivorous birds, fell to the bottom of the hole, emitting a nauseating odor and leaving a trail of maggots on the sides of that giant pit.

"Don't anyone move. Stay there a minute, goddamit," the mayordomo exclaimed as he got off his mule. A stupid feeling of guilt paralyzed the peons.

"Taiticu . . ."

"Put back that meat you stole. I saw you, goddamit! I saw you hiding it under your poncho!"

"Patroncitu mayordomu," the Indians managed to murmur in a supplicating voice that was really a confession.

"Ha ha ha. Just take out the meat. Return what you've stolen. Give it back, I say. Don't try to get around me with your stupid tricks," insisted the cholo, and, without any further comment, using his whip and fists when necessary, searched all the burial crew one by one. At each new discovery of stolen meat Policarpio warned:

"Don't let the patrón ever hear about this. Don't let him hear because he'll kill you, goddamit. You thieving Indians! You're even damned here on earth!"

And after throwing all the recovered meat into the hole, the cholo commanded:

"Alright now, sí . . . Just fill it with earth and stamp on it hard, as if it was a tapial."

"Taiticu."

"Hurry up. That's it . . . Hard . . . Harder . . ."

When the night covered the earth, Andrés Chiliquinga rose from the corner where, alongside his wife, he had awaited the pandering of the darkness in order to slither like a shadow in search of something to . . . something . . . That night he had a plan, a plan that stuck stubbornly in the hearts of all the Indians who had buried the ox. He had whispered it into Cunshi's ear, very softly so that neither the baby nor the dog could hear him and try to follow him.

Cautiously the cripple Chiliquinga crept out and closed the door. He sniffed the darkness like a dog on the trail before venturing into its mysterious heart. As he was climbing over the fence around the huasipungo, he felt the dog tangled in his feet.

"Goddam! You good-for-nothing mutt! Get inside! Take care of the woman . . . Take care of the baby . . ."

Like a small shadow, obediently, the animal took shelter in the hut while Andrés stood in the middle of the path, feeling a powerful obsession to repossess the rotten meat they had taken from him. With a bitter yet appetizing flavor in his mouth he decided to climb along the nearest short cut, on all fours, feeling his way instinctively. With the stealth of a nocturnal animal he crossed a long ditch, some chaparral, and the slippery part of the slope. In his fatigue, the images of the patrón, the mayordomo, and the priest rose in his mind. Why? Where? He hesitated a few seconds. How would they be able to find out? Who would be able to find out? The Almighty Father!

"Goddam," he muttered with clenched teeth.

But his own hunger and his family's impelled him forward, erasing all his inner fears. Soon the wind wafted an odor his way. It was the odor he was seeking. His heart galloped on a colt of morbid joy. Should he run faster? Should he be more cautious? The latter was the better idea. He assumed therefore a fearful and feline posture. His feet soon would step on the loosened earth. They would soon step on . . .

"Taiticu," he said all of a sudden.

There was a sound . . . A sound in the cursed darkness which was swallowing up everything . . . that pertrified the Indian Chiliquinga for five or ten seconds which seemed as many centuries. A sound also was sliding along the ravine, through the foliage of the enclosure, across . . . It wasn't the noise that animals make, nor that which should be made by souls in purgatory. No. Andrés strained his eyes trying to pierce the darkness. And then he discovered that . . . It was the silhouettes of a few Indians who were running from one hiding place to another across the open country. "Damn it. Goddam. Every single one has come. Even more than those of us who buried it. The blabbermouths . . . ," the Indian thought resentfully. But while he went forward, those phantoms, at first seemingly crouching and fearful, grew nearer and nearer, silently, and now without fear. They all knew, they were all prey to the same impulse. Finding himself accompanied, marching with a hungry pack, Chiliquinga lost some of his anxiety and felt lighter, swept along by a blind current. When he came to the loose earth that covered the carcass, he learned that the majority of the others had come forearmed, bringing their tools. Nervously and carefully, the shadows of his friends removed the earth with shovels and hoes. He and two or three others helped with their bare hands. When the bad odor which the earth had emitted from the very start became a fetid belch and the carcass lay exposed and in reach of the rapacious diggers, it all took place as though by magic. Hands spoke to one another in silence. And in five or ten minutes the flesh melted away. The skeleton remained, and the hide. As if someone should snatch away from them what they had won with such anxiety, they fled without delay, separating under cover of the darkness.

"Goddamit . . . I got the most tasteless meat, the softest . . . Because I failed to take along the big machete, pes . . . Stupid Indian . . . The leg was hard . . . ," Andrés Chiliquinga said to himself, feeling his theft which he had put inside his shirt, under the greasy cotton. He forthwith clambered along the slope, filled with a strange remorse, in which were blended the words and threats of the patrón, of the priest, and the sheriff. Moreover his lame foot ached at each step as it did on all dark nights. "Mama moon is after me . . . the wind spirit, too . . . ," he thought with superstitious terror. But when he came to his hut, his only haven, he opened the door violently, slammed it shut, and quickly blocked it with the weight of his fear-choked body. His was a guilty fear which could easily bring on a cruel punishment.

In feeble flames of the firelight that rose and fell, the Indian Cunshi, huddled on the floor with her baby asleep in her lap, observed her husband with a questioning glance. He did not answer. He was choked with fatigue. It was the dog who broadcast the news by sniffing as if there was something good, with his snout on high, and wagging his tail in rhythm with a happy grunt. Then Chiliquinga lifted his poncho and unbuttoned his shirt stained with blood, as if . . . "Noooo . . . It's blood and smell of beef . . . ," the wife said to herself and lost her fear.

"Ave María, taiticu."

"See . . . I'm bringing . . . Plenty . . ." said the Indian removing from his body and his bloodstained shirt a great chunk of ill-smelling meat.

"How fine, taiticu. May God reward you. Ave

María," murmured Cunshi with the ingenuous happiness of surprise, almost in tears. Quickly she got up from the floor to seize the gift that the Indian was holding out to her. At the same moment the baby awoke and the dog barked. The atmosphere in the sordid hut was suddenly alive with the assurances of satiety. The Indian woman, brave and assiduous, threw on the live coals, on two haphazardly crossed irons, everything she had received from Andrés.

Seated on the floor before the fire which at times sputtered sparks like a tallow candlewick, enveloped in smoke that smelled of burnt flesh, the Indian, his woman Cunshi, the baby and the dog—with the confidence and shamelessness of an intimate member of the family—silently savored the spectacle of the roasting meat.

"Mama . . ."

"Just wait, my Indian baby. You had your porridge . . ."

With the experience of a good cook, Cunshi took care that the meat didn't burn, turning it over each time she thought it necessary. At times she blew on the coals and, at other times, she licked her fingers, moistened with the juice of the beef, with a smacking noise of savoring delight. That was really provocative, a noise that excited the appetite of the others with an anxious urgency: the man swallowed his saliva in silence, the boy protested, the dog didn't lift his eyes from the fire. At last, when the boy, tired of waiting and of repeating "mama . . . mama . . . ," fell asleep once more, the mother took the roast from the coals, burning her hands, which she cooled as usual with her tongue. She then divided the huge chunk of meat into small pieces and served each one his ration. They ate very noisily. They devoured without perceiving the stench and the shiny sponginess of the decayed meat. Their hunger vaulted voraciously over such petty details. Except the baby who, at the second or third mouthful, fell into a deep sleep with his meat still in his little fist. The dog tried to steal the baby's meat, but the parents prevented it.

"Scat! Get out of here!"

"Scat, you good-for-nothing mutt!"

Mama Cunshi took a piece for herself and taita Andrés took another piece.

And when the Indian woman had put out the glowing embers, they all sought the straw bed—the bed laid out on the floor, behind some sticks and some dried cow dung. Andrés took off his hat and his poncho—which was all he used to take off when he went to sleep—then scratched his head in delight for all this, a delight with which he hadn't been able to scratch in a long time. As he lay down among the goat skins and old ponchos saturated with urine and filth of all kinds, he called in a low voice to his female, to his wife, to complete the refuge of the bed. The Indian woman, before obeying the man, put the dog out of the hut, fixed something on the hearth, and carried the baby to the bed—the baby who had fallen asleep in the center of the hut. And before lying down lovingly and humbly alongside her lover, for more than father and husband, he was for her a lover, she removed her shawl, the sash wound about her waist, and took off her skirt.

From the very first moment the straw bed seemed more nauseating to her than usual, the darkness more threatening, her slumber more restless. Nevertheless she slept: one, two hours. When she awoke in the silence, for it was past midnight, a painful knot was choking her throat, twisting her stomach, clutching at her bowels.

"Ayayay, taitiquitu," the woman moaned softly and then fell into a stupor which made her joints ache and the blood burn in her veins.

Andrés also awoke with a deep pain in his stomach.

Was it really paining him? Sí. And terribly. *Ay!* But
worst of all was the nausea, and the saliva like vinegar
and bitter plant juice. He managed to stay quiet. It
seemed absurd and painful to him to give back what he
had obtained with so much effort. Suddenly, because of
an irrepressible necessity that filled his mouth, the Indian
got violently to his feet, opened the door, and, a few
steps from the entrance—he couldn't go any further—
vomited everything he had eaten. All of it . . . everything. When he returned to the straw bed, a little calmer
and somewhat relieved, he heard that Cunshi, too, was
moaning:

"Ayayay, taitiquitu."

"Ave María. Your belly hurting you?"

"Arí—yes . . . yes . . ."

"Just stand it a little longer, pes. Just a little while
. . . ," advised the Indian. It seemed unjust to him that
she, too, would have to give back the food of Taita Dios.

They were both silent for long minutes—five, ten,
maybe twenty—he, struggling between the attention that
he ought to give to his female and the heaviness of a
lethargy that seemed like a weakness, and she, obedient
and credulous, suppressing her moans, her hands
clenched over her belly in a fetal attitude to withstand
the pain, to swallow the nausea which rose regularly like
a surf into her throat. And when she could no longer
stand it:

"Ayayay, taitiquitu."

"Eh, what?"

"Ayayay."

"Just stand it if you can, pes."

"Noooo . . ."

"Is it your belly?"

"Arí—yes."

"What can we do?"

"Ooooh . . ."

"Let's rub in some candle grease."

"Candle grease. Ayayay."

"A hot brick is better."

"It's better."

Groping his way, the Indian reached the hearth. From the embers and the ashes he took a brick. But, at that very instant, Cunshi, like a shadow, trembling with the nausea and the cramps, went out of the hut, and next to the fence, beneath some chilca bushes, she defecated, moaning and in a cold sweat. Before getting up, she looked at the inclement heaven covered with infite darkness and emitted a pain-laden "*ay!*" She was afraid, strangely afraid, and returned to the hut. When she fell on the straw bed, she murmured:

"Brr . . . Brrr, taitiquitu."

Andrés, who had wrapped the heated brick in a flannel cloth, offered it to the Indian woman:

"Just take it. On the belly . . . put it on your little belly . . . It's hot . . .

"Arrarray—it's hot! It's burning, pes."

"Try to stand it a little. Just a little."

The heat on her stomach reduced the cramps a little, but on the other hand it increased the lethargy and the moans. Especially her moaning. They were mingled with meaningless words and phrases. And in this way the rest of the night passed, and in this way the morning light arrived silently, filtering through the cracks and openings in the door, in the walls, in the straw roof. Instinctively Cunshi tried to get to her feet amid the tumbled ponchos and hides, but she could not. Her head, the over-all pain . . . And as she felt her strength slipping away amid clouds of insensibility, she fell sprawling on her child who was still sleeping.

"Mama, mama," the little one shrilled.

"The corn is falling down . . . The potatoes are

falling down . . . The poor Indian from the huasipungo is running . . . Ayayay . . . ," muttered the sick woman as though she were speaking to some invisible persons.

The voices awakened the Indian, who told the boy threateningly:

"You little Indian wretch. Taiticu can't sleep."

"Mama . . . Mama, pes," said the boy, excusing himself as he freed himself from the weight of his mother's body and quickly withdrew into a corner.

"Sleeping . . . the poor woman is asleep, pes. The whole damn night has been awful," thought the Indian, placing his wife's head, as loose as that of a disjointed puppet's, on a bag of filthy rags which the family used as a pillow. Then, impelled by custom, he got up, put on his poncho and sombrero, looked for the implements he needed for work, and, before going out, paralyzed by a sudden uneasy feeling, he said to himself: "No . . . She's not asleep . . . Breathing like a sick baby . . . like a diseased hen . . . like a human bewitched . . . Ave María . . . Taitiquitu . . . I'll just look at her again, pes . . ." and he went back to the straw bed, calling out:

"Cunshi. Cunshi-i-i! Does your belly still hurt you?"

The woman's silence, her half-closed eyes, her swollen mouth, the feverish laboring of her breathing, and the clayey pallor of her cheeks produced a superstitious terror in the mind of the crippled Chiliquinga, a terror that made him insist:

"Cunshi-i-i!"

The only answer was the wailing of the child who thought his father was screeching with rage as he did in the worst moments of his devilish drunken orgies.

"Just wait a second, little Indian . . . I'm not going, pes, to hit you . . . Mama's sick, I don't even know with what . . . What'll I put on you? What'll I give you?" said the Indian consoling the boy. Then he searched for something in the chinks in the walls where she used to keep herbs and amulets against the evil spirit; he looked in the corners of the hut, looked for something he didn't even know what. Tired of looking, he again came to the sick woman and murmured:

"What's hurting you, pes? Your belly? What's the matter, wife? Can't you talk? Are you asleep? Just sleep a little bit longer."

"Then turning to the boy who was watching him fearfully from a corner, he ordered:

"You, little Indian, you'll look after mama. You'll see that she doesn't get up. Take care of everything for her, pes."

"Arí—sí, taiticu," agreed the boy trying to get under the bedcovers to watch his mother better. As he lifted up the old ponchos a stench of fermented excrement saturated the hut.

"Ave María. Just like a baby my poor wife has dirtied herself; just wet herself and befouled herself. It's all one hell of a mess," lamented the Indian, and with a rag he began to clean up that latrine.

"Ayayay, taitiquitu."

"Everything's a horrible mess."

When Andrés could stand it no longer, after he had soaked up two rags and a sack, he called for the dog to help him:

"Here, dog, come here . . ."

The animal came over happily and at a sign from his master approached the straw bed and, with his voracious tongue, licked the sick woman's naked and dirty legs and buttocks.

"That's enough, goddamit!" shrieked the Indian when she began a ceaseless moaning.

"No . . . No, taitiquitu . . . Protect me, pes . . .

Taking care of me . . . Sheltering me . . . Ayayay
I . . . Poor me, I'll just run . . . Plenty . . . Ras-
cally patrún . . . No, taitiquitu . . . No, for the sake
of Taita Dius . . . Good man . . . No, pes . . . Ayayay . . ."

Without knowing why, Andrés felt he was responsible, and recalled bitterly and even remorsefully the
dogs that he hanged regularly in the hacienda patio on
the orders of the landowner or the mayordomo. Both
these personages protected the fields of young corn from
the canine plague with unrivaled zeal. As each animal
died, hanging from the rope, it protruded its dark
violet-colored tongue and, defecating and urinating,
voided its insides. "Just like Cunshi . . . Cunshi . . .
Was she about to die? No, little mama . . . Nooo . . .
Why, pes? What evil has she done, pes?" the Indian muttered to himself, dazed with fear. And he went over to the
sick woman and took her face between his hands. Fortunately, she wasn't cold like a cadaver. Just the opposite,
fever was burning in her cheeks, her lips, her eyelids, in
her whole body, in . . . That—perhaps he didn't even
realize it—reassured Chiliquinga. Then he once more
picked up the farm tools needed in his work, made it
clear to his son that he should look after his mother, and
went away as fast as he could. As always, he went along
the zigzag path. He felt stunned, tormented by an evil
omen, as though an abyss had yawned suddenly before
him, a hole into which he had fallen without reaching the
bottom because at any moment he would smash against
something or against someone that would finish him,
crush him. Mentally he reached out for some support but
found everything near him elusive, unattainable. For all
other people, for cholos, white gentlemen, and patrones,
the Indians' miseries are a mockery, despised, loathsome.
How could his anxiety over the sickness of his Indian

woman compare with the complex and delicate tragedies of the whites? It couldn't! Not at all!

"Goddamit!" Andrés cursed as he arrived at his work.

For his pains and those of his family the only answer was to sweat in the everlasting contact and the everlasting battle with the earth. Perhaps that was why on that morning the cripple Chiliquinga made the plough bite deeper than usual and whipped the yoked oxen with greater cruelty.

At noon Chiliquinga could no longer bear the painful desire to return to his huasipungo. Abandoning the oxen and everything else, without letting anyone know, because no one would have let him go—not the mayordomo, nor the Indians who watch the fields, nor the foremen—he raced up the hill, paying no heed to the cries his comrades shouted at him from the vast semi-arid countryside. When he arrived at the hovel, the boy greeted him weeping while he wailed over and over:

"Mama . . . Mamitica . . ."

"What's wrong, pes?"

"Ayayay, mama."

In the middle of the hut he discovered Cunshi, who was writhing in a horrible manner, her eyes rolling, her hair all mussed, hanging down over her shoulders, almost naked, her entire body racked like a person possessed. "It's the evil one, goddamit . . . She's possessed by the evil red devil . . . By the evil wind of the mountain . . . ," Andrés thought, if the cry deep down in his guts could be called a thought. And that superstitious obsession eliminated all possibility of a cure. Sí. It was the evil spirit who would torment her until he killed her. Impelled by a longing to dominate, by a primitive fury that refused to stand by doing nothing before the awful cruelty of the witchcraft which was torturing the poor young woman, the Indian Chiliquinga threw himself on the sick Cunshi, and with all the strength of his muscles, with all the rage in his heart, sought to suppress the diabolical spasms. But her arms, her legs, her knees, her chest, her belly, all of her was an uncontrollable tremor.

"*Longuita* . . . Wait . . . Hold on, pes . . . my sweetheart . . . ," the Indian begged.

The sick woman suddenly emitted an abortive cry, arched her body, shook her head violently, and immediately sank into a limp silence, into a mute abandonment. Since such reactions were unusual and meaningless in the habitual timidity, resignation, and meekness of the woman, Chiliquinga didn't dare to release her immediately; the demon could again seize her and shake her mercilessly. And, cautiously observing her while he waited for something to happen, he thought: "Breathing . . . she's still breathing . . . She's alive, pes . . . Taitiquitu . . . The poor thing has foamed at the mouth . . . I believe she's asleep . . . sleeping . . . Her eyes are swollen, too . . . Ave María . . . What can be done, pes? If only the wind spirit would take pity on her . . . There isn't anyone to help her . . . To reach . . ." Somewhat reassured on noting that the calm state of the woman was enduring—only very occasionally did he hear a hoarse moan—Andrés released her and huddled watchfully alongside the straw bed. And he let the hours drag by, without thinking of anything, without returning to his work, so great was his worry and his fear. At night, because of the whining urgency of his child, he looked into his bag of cold food. There wasn't much. A bit of roast corn which he gave to the little one. But the next morning —a portentous deep shadow, forerunner of a flawless dawn—the Indian, cautious and fatherly, tried to awaken the woman:

"Cunshi . . . Cunshi-i-i . . ."

She did not move, did not breathe. Why not? Maybe she was still overwhelmed by the fever and her delirium? Or there was . . . No! The gnawing of an awful suspicion unconsciously led the Indian to touch the sick woman: her face, her chest, her belly, her arms, her neck. "Taitiquitu . . . Shunguiticu . . . Cold. She's cold! Like a steel bar wet with dew, like a stone on the cold plateau, like death itself . . . ," Chiliquinga said to himself with the anguish of just having discovered an asphyxiating secret, a secret meant for him alone. No one else must know. Not the dog, nor the guinea pigs who were running hungrily from one corner of the hut to another, nor the animals of the huasipungo who were outside awaiting the Indian woman who used to feed them, nor his son who, seated by the hearth, was staring at the entrance like an idiot, nor the mayordomo who would soon learn the truth, nor the patrón who . . . "Oh! She's dead, pes. Quite dead!"

"Cunshi-i-i."

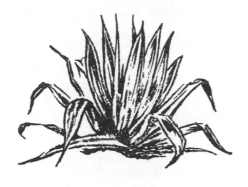

THAT VERY DAY, in the afternoon, Policarpio came to Chiliquinga's hut. From the fence he shouted:

"André-é-é-s! Why all this loafing away from work, goddamit?"

Not getting an answer, the cholo got off his mule and entered the patio of the hut. The boy and the dog—especially the dog who had felt the fury of the whip of that powerful personage many times—took shelter in the pigpen. The mayordomo spied from the hut's threshold with all the caution of a trained investigator. When his eyes became accustomed to the darkness in the hut and he could see the Indian woman's corpse on the floor and hear how the cripple Chiliquinga, huddled up next to the dead woman, was spinning phrases and tears almost silently, he realized the whole truth, and the only thing he could think of doing was to reproach and to accuse the Indian:

"It's what you deserve, dammit. For being thieves. And stupid. For being animals. You think I don't know? You ate up the carcass that the patrón ordered buried. It's a punishment from Taita Dios. The Indian José Risco, too, is writhing in his hut . . . And the woman Manuela

. . . But they said something about it soon enough . . . In time to see the curandera, pes. And now what are we going to do?"

Andrés Chiliquinga, trying to answer his visitor, raised his head heavily, looked with clouded eyes, and, in a voice stunned by despair, said:

"Not now. Oo-oo—friend mayordomo . . . Be so kind . . . Ask taiticu, patrún grande, su mercé, to advance me a little money for the wake tonight . . . Boniticu . . . Shunguiticu . . ."

Policarpio did speak about it to Don Alfonso, who refused any help to the Indian, to the thieving and disobedient Indian. Also, the mayordomo sowed the news of Cunshi's death throughout the valley and the hillsides. At once, relatives and friends of the dead woman dropped in at the huasipungo, filling the patio and the hut with sorrowful comments and anguished tears.

Just before evening, two Indian musicians, a reed player and a drummer, took their places at the head of the dead woman who lay stretched out on the floor flanked by four tallow candles burning in earthen pots. With the musicians' arrival the poorly lighted and evil-smelling hovel was filled with the monotonous, despairing beat of the native sanjuanitos. Andrés, as Cunshi's closest relative, was the one who most exalted his grief and lamented his sorrows. He mechanically took his place at the feet of the corpse, wrapped in dirty black flannel, and, huddled under his poncho, poured forth, to the beat of the music, all the choking bitterness which filled his breast. Amid a flow of mucus and tears the words gushed out:

"Ay, Cunshi, sha—gone forever."

"Ay, bonitica—lovely one, gone forever."

"Who'll take care of our little pigs, pes?"

"Why did you go away like this, without taking the little guinea pig?"

"Ay, Cunshi, gone forever."

"Ay, bonitica, gone forever."

"You left me all alone, didn't you?"

"Who'll do the sowing, pes, in our huasipungo?"

"Who'll take care, pes, of our little boy?"

"Our little boy's all alone. Ayayay . . . Ayayay . . ."

"Let's get some grass for the guinea pig."

"Let's gather some firewood on the mountain."

"Let's spend some time in the river washing our feet."

"Ay, Cunshi, gone forever."

"Ay, bonitica, gone forever."

"Who'll see, pes, if the little hen's laid an egg?"

"Who'll warm up, pes, our corn porridge?"

"Who'll start our fire, pes, on a cold night?"

"Ay, Cunshi, gone forever."

"Ay, bonitica, gone forever."

"Why've you left me all alone?"

"The little boy's crying, too."

"The dog is crying, too."

"The wind is howling, too."

"Even the little cornfield is weeping."

"The mountain is dark, too. Oh, so dark."

"The river, too, is crying."

"Ay, Cunshi, gone forever."

"Ay, bonitica, gone forever."

"Taiticu Andrés won't have no more corn, no more potatoes, no more pumpkins."

"Won't have nothing, pes, 'cause you won't sow no more."

"Because you won't look after us anymore."

"Ay, Cunshi, gone forever."

"Ay, bonitica, gone forever."

"And when we're hungry, who'll listen to our crying?"

"And when we're hurting, who'll look after our pain?"

"And when there's work to do, who'll sweat with us?"

"Ay, Cunshi, gone forever."

"Ay, bonitica, gone forever."

"Where can I go to get you new clothes?"

"A flannel skirt."

"A red shawl."

"A white kerchief."

"Why did you leave without saying goodbye? Like a stray dog."

"And in years to come, we'll have plenty to eat."

"But this year, Taita Diositu is punishing us."

"You were dying of hunger, pes, but you said nothing, nothing."

"Ay, Cunshi, gone forever."

"Ay, bonitica, gone forever."

With his lips dry, his eyes burning, his throat choked up, his soul lacerated, the Indian went on bewailing, to the rhythm of the music, his wife's excellent qualities, her small desires—never realized—and her quiet virtues. Before his own people he could say everything. They, too . . . They, when they saw he was exhausted, hoarse, and drained of tears, dragged him to a corner of the hut, gave him a good dose of brandy to numb his grief, and left him lying limp as a rag, moaning throughout the night. Then some others who felt they had the right, as a member of the family, as godparent, or as a close friend, replaced Andrés Chiliquinga with their laments, their cries, and their weeping at the corpse's feet. Each one followed in turn and in a veritable competition of moaning. The moans little by little were heightened until at dawn they blended into a chorus that resembled the howl of a bleeding beast corraled midway between the indifference of the craggy earth and that of heaven, where the monotonous music of the sanjuanitos filtered in to veil their anguish.

"The wake of poor Cunshi," said the farmers, crossing themselves when from afar they heard that grieving murmur which flowed over the hillside in a viscous blob of mourning.

"The wake that soothes."

"The wake that says goodbye."

"The chasquibaaay."

Andrés didn't stop drinking. It was as if he wanted to drown a hate without rudder or compass, a hate that drifted aimlessly deep within him and, which after so much searching for an appropriate target, could find no victim but himself.

After three days, the wake ended in an aura of putrescence—the fetid smell of the decaying body, the stinking odors of the alcoholic breaths, the hoarseness and weariness. Then they spoke of the jachimayshay: the bathing of the corpse to speed it on its eternal journey.

"Yes, taiticu."

"Yes, boniticu."

"Poor Cunshi is asking for it."

"Jachimayshay. Jachimayshay!" demanded friends and relatives, as if they had suddenly noticed the presence of a strange visitor.

With some old sticks, some found in the hut, others brought in by someone, the most skillful Indians at the wake erected a type of scaffold on which they placed Cunshi's rigid and ill-smelling body. Reciting ancient prayers in Quichua, they carried the corpse to the bank of the river for the ritual of the jachimayshay. After washing their face and hands a group of women removed the clothes from the dead Cunshi and bathed her carefully. They scrubbed her with frothy pads made of the agave plant, scraped the calluses on the heels with fragments of brick, and removed all the head lice with a comb made of horn. She must take her ultimate trip as clean as she was on the day she was born.

Andrés, on the other hand, almost at the very hour his friends and relatives were busy with the jachimayshay, entered the parish priest's house in the town, to deal with the priest about the costs of the mass, the responsories, and the Christian burial.

"At last . . . I was wondering why you hadn't been to see me at such a trying time. Poor Cunshi," chanted the cassocked one as soon as he saw the Indian.

"How could you imagine I wouldn't come, pes, taitiquitu, su mercé?"

"Of course. That's what I like to hear. She was so good. So accommodating she was."

"May God bless you for that, amitu. Now I am here to ask, su mercé, how much it will cost for the mass, the responsories, the burial—for everything."

"Well, let's see now . . ."

"Patroncitu."

"Come . . . Come along with me . . . The mass and the responsories are a customary thing in such affairs. But with regard to the burial you'll have to see what you like best, what you're ready to pay. In this you have complete liberty. Absolute liberty," the priest murmured jovially as he guided the Indian through the pillars of the porch of his house and past the supports that propped up the walls of the dilapidated church. When they came to a kind of a field of graves, blossoming with crosses, which extended behind the temple, the priest commanded his customer:

"Look . . . My son, look at this."

"Jesus. Ave María," said Chiliquinga respectfully taking off his hat.

"Look!" insisted the priest, contemplating his cemetery with the greedy eyes of a landowner: according to some evil rumors it was his richly-sown field.

"Sí, taiticu. I'm looking, pes."

"Well, now. These who are buried here, in the first rows, since they are closer to the high altar, closer to the prayers, and therefore closer to our Holy Lord," the priest mechanically took off his hat and lowered his eyes, with a mystical bow, "are the ones who get to heaven soonest, the ones who are usually saved. Well . . . From here to heaven it's only a short step! Look . . . look closely," the priest insisted, pointing out to the dazed Indian the crosses on the first row of graves. At the foot of each grave there grew violets, geraniums, and carnations. Then, placidly leaning against a cypress tree, he continued to extol the virtues of his merchandise like a market woman hawking her vegetables:

"The very air is peaceful, even its fragrance is from heaven, and its whole aspect is blissful. Everything just breathes virtue. Can't you smell it?"

"Taiticu."

"Right now I'd like to have a heretic in front of me who would dare say that these flowers could ever grow in a human garden. Why, from here it's just a tiny step to heaven."

Then the priest paused, looked at the Indian, who seemed timid, deep in thought, and humble before such an extraordinary thing for his poor wife, advanced along a short path, and continued his sermon in front of the crosses on the graves arising in the center of the cemetery:

"These unpainted wooden crosses belong to the poor cholos and Indians. As you can easily understand they are a little far from the sanctuary, and the prayers sometimes reach them and sometimes don't. God's mercy, which is infinite" (the priest made another bow and another salute with his birreta and with his eyes) "has destined these unhappy souls to go to Purgatory. You, my dear Chiliquinga, know what the tortures of Purgatory are like. They're worse than those of Hell."

Noting that the Indian lowered his eyes as if ashamed that the merchandise he could afford would be so shabbily dealt with, the good minister of God hastened to console him:

"But they'll be saved nevertheless. One of these days, that is. It's just like these rose bushes here: a little neglected, almost smothered by the weeds, but . . . It has been very hard for them to rid themselves of the thorns and brambles . . . But finally, one day they'll bloom, give off their perfume."

After saying this he walked on a few steps and, becoming serious, with an apocalyptic tone and gesture stated:

"And finally . . ."

The priest interrupted his discourse when he saw that the Indian was entering an area of badly neglected graves, crumbling and covered with damp moss and gray lichens.

"Don't go any farther!" he shouted.

"Jesus, taiticu."

"Don't you notice a strange odor? Kind of fetid? Like sulphur?"

"No, su mercé, I don't," Chiliquinga replied after sniffing on all sides."

"Oh! Then you are not in God's grace. And naturally anyone who is not in God's grace can't . . ."

The Indian felt a somber weight draining his strength. With a trembling clumsy movement he concentrated his efforts on twirling his hat in his hands.

Meanwhile the señor priest, with a glance of disdain and loathing, pointed toward the far corner of the cemetery where there was nothing but worm-eaten crosses, where the nettles, brambles, and hawthorns had grown like a witch's tangled hair, and where a ceaseless buzzing of bumblebees and mosquitoes chilled one's spirit.

"Amitu . . ."

"Over there . . . the distant ones . . . the forgotten ones . . . the reprobates."

"Oooo, ay . . ."

"Those who are in . . ."

As if the word was burning his mouth the priest spat out:

". . . Hell!"

On hearing that word, the Indian tried to leave the priest by running away, panic stricken like one who suddenly finds he has been, unknowingly, teetering on the edge of an abyss.

"Calm yourself, my son, calm yourself . . . ," admonished the minister blocking Andrés' flight. But nonetheless he felt bound to conclude:

"Can't you hear that clamor? Don't you smell that fetid odor? Can't you see that it's a macabre nightmare?"

"Taiticu."

"That's the smell, the wailing, and the putrefaction of condemned souls."

"Sí, boniticu."

With his customer thus prepared, the cassocked one readied himself to discuss the economics of the affair:

"Now . . . Of course . . . As you've always been a faithful servant I'm going to make you a bargain. And that's something I've never done for anybody. For the mass, the responsories, and burial in the first row I'll charge you only thirty-five sucres. I'm giving it away! Now for burial in the center section, which I think will really be most suitable, it'll cost just twenty-five sucres."

"And what about . . . ?"

"Oh, in the last rows where only the demons reside, it's five sucres. Something I could never recommend to you even if I went crazy. It would be better to leave the woman unburied. But since it's a work of charity to bury the dead, it must be done."

"Sí, taiticu."

"Now you know . . ."

"Taiticuuu," the Indian tried to object.

"Just think a while before you say anything. It's only natural that all the prayers not needed by those buried in the first row are helping those in the second row. But nothing is left over to reach those in the third row. It just can't get to them at all. After all, what is thirty-five sucres compared to eternal life? Nothing at all! What is twenty-five sucres if there's a real hope to save a soul?"

"All right, pes, taiticu. It'll be the first row, pes."

"Now you're talking. I didn't think you'd take anything else."

"But, taiticu. Show me, pes, a little charity."

"You mean lower the price? That's what the middle row is for. Poor Cunshi will have to suffer a little longer but she'll be saved. Yes, she'll be saved."

"No. God keep her. I didn't mean a lower price. I just wanted you to trust me a while, pes."

"Eh? What did you say?"

"A little credit, that's all. I can pay you off in work. Anything you want, taiticu. I'll just come at four in the morning to sow or to plow . . ."

"No! Impossible!" Then the priest, really indignant, thought to himself, "Get into heaven on credit. That's the last straw. And if the Indian doesn't pay me here on earth who'll get it out of the dead woman up there?" Then he continued:

"It can't be done. It would be stupid. To mix vulgar earthly transactions with heavenly affairs. My God! What is it I hear? What offense are they trying to inflict on You now, Lord?"

As the priest at this moment started to raise his arms and eyes to heaven, following his usual manner of chatting with the Celestial Court, the Indian hurriedly implored:

"Don't, taiticu. Don't raise your arms . . ."

"Then what's your answer? Thirty-five, twenty-five . . ."

"Now, taiticu . . . I don't . . ."

"In the next world everything is on a cash basis."

"So be it, pes. Then I'm going to raise the money, pes. May the Almighty Father help me, pes."

"You'll just have to get it wherever you can. The salvation of a soul comes first, especially the soul of a beloved person. Poor Cunshi's soul. Such a good woman she was. So dutiful . . . ," said the priest assuming a mournful expression and emitting a deep sigh.

WHEN ANDRÉS returned to the hut, his relatives, his friends, his son, and even his dog lay piled up in the corners, snoring. The dead woman, on the other hand, with her nauseating stench, cried aloud for burial. Nervous and hopeless before that urgency, Chiliquinga again lost himself among the zigzag paths on the mountain slope. With his gait, at times slow, at times quick like that of a drunkard—drunk with hopes, drunk with projects, drunk with the demands and the words of the priest—he avoided, seemingly unconsciously, meeting anybody. He had no purpose. No one could help him. Nobody! Get . . . Get the money . . . Even what was drunk up during the wake had been brought by the people who came to weep and assuage their grief. Suddenly, he thought of an equivalent that could cover the expenses of the burial. He could sell something. What? Nothing of value was left in the huasipungo. He could ask someone for a loan. Who? His debt to the hacienda was very large. In fact, he didn't know how . . . It would take years of labor to pay it off . . . Perhaps his whole life . . . And according to the mayordomo the patrón was angry. But he could . . . Steal! That infernal temptation stopped the Indian in his tracks. He then began to mutter strange things under his breath, searching, with eyes on the ground, for something that undoubtedly he expected to see suddenly appear before him: among the garbage along the road, among the cacti growing along the walls, in the ruts cut in the mud by the carts, in the heaven . . . "Heaven for my Cunshi. Goddam. With what money, pes?" An inner voice shouted from his very bowels: "Impossible!"

In the distance, beyond the river pasture, the Indian herdsmen and hacienda servants were enclosing the patrón's cattle in the fenced area. "Oo-oo . . . Five o'clock . . ." thought Chiliquinga, watching the brown stain of the cattle smear across the valley, and believed he had unconsciously found a fragment of hope on which to lean his despair. On a fragment of hope? What could it be? He lost its trail but drew in new courage with a deep sigh, and then went on along a path that bordered the edge of a ravine. The sun had set and the afternoon ripened into night among cottony shreds of fog. Tired of walking, Chiliquinga asked himself where he was going and, leaning against a fence, muttered under his breath:

"Why all this running around, all this going about, pes? Because I'm just stupid . . . Just naturally doing wrong . . . That's exactly how I am . . . Good for nothing . . . Who's going to sympathize, pes? Who'll show charity, pes? Goddamit!"

Suddenly a strange presence behind him sent a shiver through his exhausted spirit. "The breath of papa devil," he told himself, looking obliquely behind him. It was . . . It was the head of a cow who was stretching her snout over the wall of cactus sniffing for some tender grass.

"Ave María, I was almost frightened, pes . . . ," muttered the Indian and jumped over the wall to see the animal better. It was a cow wearing the hacienda's brand. "How can it be, pes? The herdsman drove them all off . . . But they left the cow all alone . . . She's a smart one . . . The mayordomo . . . The patrún . . . Uuuy . . . ," thought Chiliquinga as he climbed up a cliff from where he could shout to the people in the valley to come back to look for the lost animal. But a crystal-clear thought kept him from crying out. He would be able to . . . He hesitated a few seconds. He looked about him. Nobody there. Besides the fog and the twilight were thickening with each passing moment. A cow is worth . . . "Oo-oo . . . But was it heaven-sent by Taita Dius or was it a temptation of taita diablu . . . Which one sent it, pes?" the Indian asked himself, sliding down from the rock he had wanted to climb. Everything was right, everything was easy. The solitude, the silence, the night.

"May God reward You, Taita Diositu," said Andrés gratefully, accepting God's help without any pangs of conscience. Yes. He'd steal the cow to speed Cunshi on to heaven. The solution was clear. He would go to the village on the other side of the hill where no one knew him. He waited for the night and then, driving the cow ahead, he went down the road.

The next day at dawn Andrés Chiliquinga returned from his adventure. Things had changed for him. He had ten five-sucre bills hidden in the sash wrapped around his waist.

A few days later the roads in the valley and the twisting mountain paths were crawling with inquiries and investigations:

"The patroncitu says it cost one hundred sucres."

"A hundred whole sucres."

"How can it be fair to make a poor Indian pay for it?"

"Like a herdsman, pes."

"Or a servant at the patrón's house, pes."

"Or a caretaker, pes."

"The cow could be lost."

"The cow could be stolen."

"The big cow."

"The spotted cow."

"Blaming a poor Indian for it!"

"Who would dare to do it."

"Who can the thief be?"

"He'll be out of luck."

"He'll be punished by Taita Dius."

Meanwhile, guided by the sensitive noses of the dogs, by the hoof marks, and by the flaming torch light which like a red banner and like a devilish compass floated at the tip of a burning stick, the pursuers relentlessly followed the thief's tracks.

"Over here, goddamit."

"Over on the other side, too."

"Ave María."

"The dogs . . . Let the dogs loose . . ."

"Compare the footprints."

"Are they made by Indian sandals?"

"Are they made by a white man's shoes?"

"Looks like an Indian's."

"Jesus Christ!"

"God look after him!"

After a two-day investigation the truth came out. Since the criminal couldn't return the stolen cow nor its worth in cash, and since the priest alleged the impossibility of negotiation and restitution with the things of God in Heaven, they charged one hundred sucres to the guilty man's debit side of his huasipungo account.

But in addition, Don Alfonso thought it necessary to give the Indians a lesson that would strengthen their moral fibre, so that the gringo gentlemen, when they came, wouldn't be annoyed by their corrupt practices. Yes, that was it. A public punishment to be administered in the patio of the hacienda.

"The Indians will see with their own eyes that theft, laziness, and lack of respect for their master's property can only lead to an exemplary show of authority, to punishment, to the tortures of the whip," Don Alfonso proclaimed to the sheriff who was ready to carry out his sacred duties with all precision.

"Just as you say, pes. These Indian dogs will rob you of your very existence. Where could they ever find another master as good as you?"

"And that's why I'm going to wash my hands of all this. The gringos will be coming soon. I only hope that at the hands of those dominating men, who have succeeded so masterfully in pulling the cart of civilization, these almost savage Indian bandits will learn how to behave. I don't want to be their victim any longer."

"Then you're really going to leave us?"

"And what else can I do?" the landowner questioned

in his turn, with a martyr-like gesture of resignation.

"That's bad, pes."

"I've even delayed a little in turning over the hacienda—for sentimental reasons. The land really gets a strong hold on you. Strong! The places where we've worked and suffered always appeal more to us than those where we've only enjoyed ourselves."

The patio of the hacienda was jammed with Indians. They had come to watch the punishment of Andrés Chiliquinga. Some had come willingly, others had almost been forced to come. From one of the sheds which surrounded the house they brought out the victim—crestfallen, his eyes darting sideways, his hands and his fear huddled beneath his poncho. His son—now orphaned of Cunshi—with the ingenuousness of his tender years, proudly marched behind his father, flanked by the rural policemen from the sheriff's office who were guarding the Indian criminal. The men who were going to participate in the spectacle walked to the center of the patio, next to the stake—really a tree trunk—where the herdsmen tamed the fury of the cattle, where they branded the hacienda's cattle, where they tied up the cows to be milked for the first time, and where they hung the dogs who invaded the fields of tender corn.

"Bring him over here!" commanded Jacinto Quintana, who had the role of master of ceremonies.

The thief was dragged to the sheriff's feet by two policemen. As though everything had been foreseen and ordained, they stripped him of his poncho and his shirt amid the general silence. Doubtless no one cared to miss a single detail. Naked down to his navel, his two thumbs were then tied with a thong.

"See that everything's good and tight. I don't want him to break loose and run away. Take the other end and run it over the stake," Jacinto Quintana commanded with the air of a great leader and in a hoarse voice made more raucous by the expectant silence.

Obediently, the police and the prudent Indian house servants threw the thong over the open fork at the top of the stake. At the first tug by the bailiffs, the arms and naked back of the Indian were stretched skyward, as though entreating heaven.

"Pull hard! With strength, goddamit!" shrieked the sheriff when he saw that the men who were pulling were unable to hoist the luckless Indian.

"Now, cholitos, when I count one."

"On-n-n-e!"

When at last he was dangling in the air, Andrés Chiliquinga's bones creaked lightly, and the leather thong became taut as a string on a guitar.

At each movement of his body Andrés Chiliquinga felt a bite of fire in his thumbs. In the crowd's mind there floated, with an unconscious vagueness, the sad impression of finding themselves confronted with their own destiny. At that moment the sheriff, after spitting on his hands to insure his hold on the whip and, at an imperative gesture by Don Alfonso Pereira, who was presiding over that "court of justice" from the porch of his house, began to beat the Indian.

The whiplashes crackled across the furtive silence of the multitude. The moans of the victim muted the spectators even more than the cracks of the whip, stifling the ferment of an ill-defined vengeance: "Why, taiticu? Why does it always have to be the poor Indian? Goddam! It's an accursed world! In his mouth the bitter juice of the bramble berry, in his heart the devil's own bile. Just bear it, taiticu, writhing like a worm trod under foot. So that later . . . What, pes? Nothing, goddamit . . ."

From a corner where he had remained forgotten, and with a cat-like spring, Cunshi's son darted toward the legs of the man who was whipping his father and sank his teeth into his thigh like a mad dog.

"Ayayay, ouch! Let go!"

"Oo-oooo . . ."

"You Indian sonofabitch!" shrieked Jacinto Quintana when he discovered the child, anchored to his flesh by his teeth.

"Hit him with the whip! Quick! Let him learn to become humble right now when he's still a child!" the master ordered, going down to the lowest step, at the very moment when the assaulted sheriff freed himself from the boy by flinging him to the ground with a shove and a lash of the whip.

"Goddam! Indian thief!"

The sheriff, the police, and the house servants tamed the child with blows. The weeping and shouts of the orphan sowed in the throng an anxiety to plead: "Enough, goddamit! Enough!" But the protest was dissipated in resignation and fear, leaving only a slight whisper of tears and sniffling by the women.

The whip once more fell across Chiliquinga's back. No one was capable of again interrupting the sacred labor.

"Indian sonofabitch! He gave in quickly enough. The weakkneed sissy!"

In the solitude of their hut, father, and son cured their wounds with a curious mixture of brandy, urine, tobacco, and salt.

FROM MOUTH to mouth the news of the gringos' arrival ran through the village.

"They're bringing plenty of money, girls."

"To spread around."

"Ha-ha-ha!"

"They say they're quite generous."

"Only hope they do away with this famine we're enduring."

"They say they'll make improvements in the village."

"We'll have to go out to meet them."

"What'll they give us?"

"What'll they bring us?"

"They'll be coming up through here."

"Luchita-a-a-a!"

"At your service."

"You'll sweep in front of the store. These people shouldn't see all the garbage out there."

"They're bringing machines along."

"That's what they say."

"That's what they report."

"More than twenty, according to Jacinto."

"That's swell, pes."

"They're bringing money, mama."

"Hooray for the gringos!"

"Hooray!"

All the flags in the village adorned doors and windows—a custom of the capital city for national holidays and for the celebrations of the Heart of Jesus and of the Sorrowing Virgin. The marriageable peasant women combed their hair that day with camomile water to lighten it, and they put loud-colored ribbons in their hair and around their necks.

At the critical hour everyone in the village thronged to the plaza to hear the good news: the priest and the sexton from the church tower, the women from the doorways of their stores, the old women and the men from their porches facing the road, and from the street, mounted on sticks or reed horses, the boys.

Unfortunately, the gringo gentlemen, without noticing the anxiety of the people nor the adornments in the village, passed through it at full speed in three luxurious automobiles. And so the applause, the hurrahs, and the general festivity were stifled. Among the villagers there remained only the memory:

"I saw a man with blond hair."

"Blond like an angel's."

"I saw him, too."

"All of us saw him."

"They looked like Taita Dios."

"Wonder what their wives are like."

"Wonder what their babies are like."

"Wonder if they drink brandy."

"Wonder what they get drunk on."

"They didn't stop here as we thought."

"Why should they, pes?"

"They didn't speak to us."

"Why would they want to speak, pes, with us poor peasants?"

"That's what . . ."

"What would you have said to them?"

"Me, I . . ."

"What would you have offered them?"

"They went straight out to the patrón Alfonso Pereira."

"Of course they went to him, pes."

"Sure, he has what . . ."

"It's all between them."

"Everything."

Standing on an adobe wall, Don Alfonso, Mr. Chapy, and two other gringos were planning, in pleasant conversation as they viewed the vast expanse of the mountain, the rough sketch for their great projects.

"The river project is in good shape. A great work. We'll build our houses and our offices over there," announced one of the foreigners.

"Very well . . . good," said the other.

"The road isn't so bad, either."

"When I promise something, I keep my word," replied Don Alfonso, filled with pride.

"That's how to do business."

"I've had to put in a lot of care, a lot of skill, and a lot of money."

"Oh, a magnificent job, my friend."

"Thank you."

"But, look over there . . . On that hill we'll put up the big sawmill. We want it cleaned off . . . that's all we need . . ." said Mr. Chapy pointing to the hillside on which the improvised huasipungos of the Indians displaced from the riverbank were now clinging.

"Ah, that . . . ," muttered Don Alfonso in a doubtful voice which seemed to imply: "I didn't agree to do all that."

"It's not very much. The greater part of it . . ."

"Is already done."

"Yes, but . . . That has to be done, too."

"It will be," the landowner concluded, a little annoyed. Then, changing the subject of the chat, he said "On this side we have, as you can see, enough forests to last a century. The timber . . ."

"That's something else. We are going to be engaged in an altogether different thing. You didn't read that the eastern range of the Andes is full of oil. You and your uncle will realize a good profit in the deal."

"Sí. Of course . . ."

"The timber business is just to begin with . . . So that we're not bothered by . . ."

"Oh, there won't be any trouble that way. Here you're perfectly safe. No one would dare bother you. Who would? Who'd be able to? After all, you . . . You've brought civilization here. What else do the Indians want?" said Pereira, aiming a kick at the pedestal of earth that supported him. But as the wall was an old one it crumbled, unable to withstand such a display of force, and the landowner, with all his pomposity, crashed to the ground amid clouds of dust.

"You see? You see how we don't even know the very ground we walk on?"

Keeping to his part of the agreement with the gringo gentlemen, Don Alfonso Pereira hired a few rural outlaws to dislodge the Indians from the hillside huasipungos. The outlaw group was headed by One-Eyed Rodríguez and by Jacinto Quintana's policemen. Employing the cunning tactics of surprise and abuse, these men fell on the first hut: good practice for the rest of the huts.

"Get out! You've got to get out of here at once!" One-Eyed Rodríguez commanded from the doorway of the first hut, addressing an Indian woman who at that moment was grinding corn on a stone and two boys who were shooing off the hens to keep them from the corn.

As would be expected the three thus addressed, faced with the shock of such an order, remained petrified, without knowing what to say, what to do, or how to answer. Only the dog, a small, skinny and suspicious animal, dared to reply with a long and doleful howl.

"You're not going to obey the patrón's orders?"

"Taiticu . . ." murmured the Indian woman and the two boys, transfixed, unable to move.

"You won't?"

As no one answered this time, the one-eyed cholo, turning to the armed policemen who were with him, said in the voice of one looking for corroboration:

"It's plain to see. You are witnesses. They are rebelling."

"That's just what it is, pes."

"Just get on with your duty. Drag them out!"

"Get them out fast, goddamit!

"Now is when we begin the jobs which the gringo gentlemen ordered done."

"Taiticu-u-us."

At that moment from the darkest corner of the hovel came an Indian of medium height and worried eyes. With a voice of timid supplication he protested:

"Why are you moving us out, pes? It's my huasipungo. Since the times of the great patrón himself. My huasipungo!"

Varying were the answers that the Indian received from the group of cholos going on with their destructive labor, even if they all were in agreement:

"We don't know nothing, goddamit."

"Go on out . . . Just go on out!"

"Get out!"

"Up on the mountain there's land and to spare."

"This land is needed by the patrón."

"Everybody, get out!"

As the Indian tried to protest the forced removal of his family, one of the men gave him a shove which sent him sprawling over the stone where the woman was grinding the corn. Meanwhile, the others, armed with picks, crowbars and shovels, began their work on the hut.

"Everybody, out!"

"Patroncitu. For charity's sake, for your own life, for your saintly souls. Just wait a little bit longer, pes," implored the Indian trembling half with fear and half with rage.

"For Taita Dius. For Mama Virgin," pleaded the Indian woman.

"Oo-oo-oo . . . ," shrilled the two boys.

"Get out, goddamit!"

"Just a little while so we can take out the goat skins, take out the old ponchos, take out the earthenware pot, take everything out," entreated the Indian accepting the misfortune as an inevitable thing; he knew that confronted by the patron's edict, by One-Eyed Rodríguez' whip, and by the sheriff's bullets nothing could be done.

Hurriedly the woman took out everything she could from the hut amid the shouting and crying of the children. Before the very eyes of the Indian family the thatched roof was smashed by machete blows and the adobe walls, blackened on the inside, crumbling on the outside, were demolished by crowbar and pick.

In spite of knowing all he did about the "amo, su mercé, patrón grande," the Indian filled with ingenuousness and a stupid hope, like an automaton, didn't stop warning:

"I'll tell the patrún, dammit . . . The patrún grande . . . The patrún will see we get justice."

"He'll kick you out, you Indian savage. He's the one who sent us. Why do you think we're here, pes?" said the men as they withdrew leaving everything reduced to rubble.

Amid the rubbish and the dust, the woman and the boys, moaning and weeping as at a wake, searched not once, but over and over for anything they could carry away with them:

"Look at the flannel cloth, ayayay."

"The wooden spoon, too."

"The earthenware cooking pan."

"Every single thing looks so damn forlorn."

"The baby's swaddling cloth."

"A woman's shawl."

"The grinding stone because it's so heavy will just have to stay here."

"The adobe pillows, too."

"The dried cow dung, ayayay."

"Search well, baby."

"Search well, mama."

"Ayayayay."

The Indian, perhaps crazed with grief, without even venturing to pick up anything, walked a few times among the sticks, the straws, the heaps of earth that still stank of the misery of his bedding, of his food, his sweat, of his drunken orgies, and of his lice. An asphyxiating and trembling anxiety throbbed in his gut: What to do? Where to go? How could he uproot himself from that piece of earth which up till a few minutes ago he had believed his?

In the afternoon, slipping into a resignation about to turn into tears or into curses, the Indian made bundles of everything that his family had salvaged, and followed by his wife, by his boys, and by the dog, he set out on the mountain path, hoping to find lodging with his friend Tocuso until he could speak with the patrón.

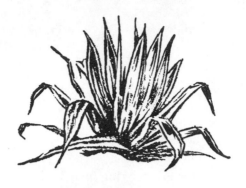

ONE OF HIS NEIGHBORS, hurriedly going along the path that passed by Andrés Chiliquinga's hut, was the first to tell him of the news of the violent dispossessing of the huasipungos on the hillside.

"This whole side of the hill is going to be cleaned off, taiticu."

"What are you saying, pes?"

"Arí, that's it."

"The ones down below?"

"The ones down below."

That was disquieting, very disquieting, but the Indian felt reassured because it seemed impossible to him that they'd reach the summit where he and the dead Cunshi had built their cabin which now . . . But by mid-morning, his son, who had gone down to the river for water, came running back and, between gasps of fatigue and fright, told him:

"They're knocking down the hut of our neighbor Cachitambu, taiticu."

"What's that?"

"Right next to us, pes. The sheriff said they're coming to tear down this one too."

"What?"

"Arí, yes, taiticu."

"My hut?"

"Arí, he said . . ."

"Take away Chiliquinga's huasipungo?"

"Arí, taiticu."

"You little liar."

"Arí, taiticu. I was there listening, pes."

"Goddamit, shit!"

"We still have to get the huasipungo of the cripple Andrés, they were saying."

"The cripple Andrés, eh?"

"Arí, taiticu."

"Goddamit!"

"It's true."

"They're not going to steal it just like that from taita Andrés Chiliquinga," concluded the Indian scratching his head, filled with an awakening of brooding and ill-defined thoughts of vengeance. It was no longer impossible to doubt the truth of the outrage which had invaded the hillside. They were coming . . . They'd be coming sooner than he could even imagine. They'd knock down his roof; they'd take away his land. Unable to come up with any possible defense, trapped as always, he turned pale, his mouth half open, his eyes staring, his throat knotted. No! It seemed ridiculous that he . . . They'd have to fell him with an axe like a sturdy tree on the mountain. They'd have to drag him off with a yoke of oxen to uproot him from his hut to which he had adapted himself, where he had seen his baby born and his Cunshi die. Impossible! It was a lie! Nevertheless, along all the twisting mountain paths the tragic news caused a disturbance akin to sullen protests or to repressed hate. Beneath an inclement heaven, and wandering aimlessly, the despoiled Indians rolled up their ponchos in a fighting manner as if they were drunk; something was boiling in their blood, burning in their eyes, making their fingers twitch; it crackled between their teeth like toast made of oaths. The Indian women muttered strange things, blew their noses noisily, and from time to time emitted a howl as they recalled the stark reality they were living. The children were crying. Perhaps the worry of those who were awaiting the tragic visit was more anguished and stifled. The men went in and out of their huts, looked for something in their pigsties, in their chicken coops, in their tiny fields; they sniffed in all the corners, they pounded their chests with their fists—a strange, masochistic aberration—and threatened the calm of the heavens with the rage of an unreasoning beast. The women, by the side of their fathers or their husbands who could protect them, planned and demanded things that were absurdly heroic. The boys armed themselves with sticks and stones which in the end would prove useless. And everything on the hillside, with its small streams, with its wide ravines, with its crazy zigzag paths, with its colors—some vivid, others dull—seemed to palpitate like a sickly mass in the middle of the valley.

Hoping for something providential, the Indian throng, their lips dry and their eyes burning, searched the horizon. It must be coming from somewhere! But from where, goddamit? From . . . From very far away, apparently. From the very heart of the thick cactus plants, from the chaparral, from the craggy mountain top. From a mysterious horn which some one was blowing to gather the Indians together and arouse their ancestral spirit of rebellion. Yes, it had arrived. It was Andrés Chiliquinga who had climbed to the top of his huasipungo fence—on the counsel and impulse of the sheer fury of his despair—and who was rallying his people with the hoarse voice of the battle horn he had inherited from his father.

The huasipungueros on the hilltop—in ambush, like poisonous larvae—awoke then with a cry that shook the valley. Up the paths, along the mountain short-cuts, and through the roads raced the naked feet of the Indian women and children, and the fibre and rope sandaled feet of their men. The Indians' disconcerted and defenseless attitude changed abruptly at the enchantment wrought by that ancestral cry which reached them from Chiliquinga's huasipungo with all the vigor of an assault on a barricade.

From every edge of the hillside and even from below swarmed the Indians with their women, their babies, and their dogs to Andrés Chiliquinga's huasipungo. They arrived sweating, trembling with rebellion, their faces dripping hatred and their eyes blazing with hopeful questions:

"What'll we do, goddamit?"

"Yes, what?"

"And how?"

"Just tell us, taiticu Andrés!"

"Tell us what to set fire to—anything!"

"Tell us who to kill!"

"Goddam!"

"Speak up, pes!"

"It's not right for you to say nothing after sounding the horn of our great ancestors!"

"Taiticuuu!"

"You've got to say something!"

"You must advise us—something!"

"Why, pes, did you gather all the poor Indians like a flock of sheep?"

"Yes, what for?"

"Why didn't you just leave us with our grief like our ancestors before us?"

"Now our hearts are bitten by hope."

"Wandering across hill and ravine."

"Why, goddamit?"

"So now, speak up, pes."

"What does the battle horn say?"

"Wha-a-a-at?"

"Taiticuuu!"

"Are they going to remove us just like this from our lands?"

"From our huts, too?"

"From our little fields, too?"

"From every thing we possess?"

"They'll pull us out of here just like weeds."

"Like a stray cur."

"Tell us, pes!"

"Taiticuuu."

Andrés felt very strongly the crowd's urgent attitude, which was also his own. The crowd filled the patio of his huasipungo and swarmed back of his fence, bristling with questions, picks, axes, machetes, sticks, and with clenched fists raised on high. Andrés felt all this so strongly that he thought he was falling into a bottomless pit, that he would die of shame and confusion. Why indeed had he summoned all his neighbors with that unconscious urgency he had felt coursing through his veins? What should he tell them? Who had really given him that idea? Was it merely a criminal caprice of his blood, the blood of a half-tamed and insolent Indian? No! Some one or something made him remember at that very moment that he was reacting in this way guided by the profound attachment for his piece of land and for the roof over his head, instinctively impelled by a wholesome anger against injustice. And then it was that Chiliquinga, still perched on his wall, clenched his fingers on the horn from which had burst the rebellious cries, and, sensing with a clear and infinite eagerness the desire and urgency of the Indians, hit upon the slogan which was to give them a banner and arouse their blind emotions. He shouted until he was hoarse:

"Ñucanchic huasipungooo! Our huasipungos belong to us!"

"Ñucanchic huasipungo!" the crowd howled, raising their fists and weapons on high with a fervor that reached them from long ago, from their remotest Inca ancestors. The cry rolled down the hill, knifed through the mountain, whirled across the valley, and ultimately pierced the heart of the group of houses of the hacienda:

"Ñucanchic huasipungo!"

The rustic throng, growing larger and more violent with the addition of Indians from the entire region, bearing before them the deafening shout given to them by Chiliquinga, flowed down the zigzag mountain paths. The more daring and impatient Indians, to hurry their descent, threw themselves on the ground and rolled down the slope. At the passage of that infernal caravan all the silences of the chaparral, the gullies, and the side ditches fled as though by magic; the fields shuddered and heaven's own countenance became wrinkled.

In the midst of that brown stain which advanced, seemingly slowly, the women, dishevelled and dirty, followed by a multitude of bare-bellied and bare-bottomed children, shrieked forth their wails and made known some shameful outrage of the white men in order to incite more and more the anger and hatred of their males.

"Ñucanchic huasipungo!"

The children, imitating the older Indians, armed with branches, sticks, and logs, not knowing where their shouting would lead them, cried out repeatedly:

"Ñucanchic huasipungo!"

The furious huasipungueros' first clash was with a group of men led by One-Eyed Rodríguez which had been joined by Jacinto Quintana. Their bullets stopped the Indians. Realizing the danger, the sheriff tried to flee through a gorge, but unfortunately, along the bottom of that same ravine sprouted some Indians who were following Andrés Chiliquinga. With his lameness apparently supported on the crutch of a crazed fury, Andrés sprang on the cholo and, with a diabolic strength and violence, cancelled the entire debt of his vengeance, raining blows of his eucalyptus club on the head of the dazed sheriff. The cholo fell with a "goddamit" and quickly tried to push himself erect with his hands.

"Accursed one!" angrily snorted the chorus of Indians with the satisfaction of having crushed a louse which had been sucking their blood ever since they could remember.

The sheriff, stunned by the blow, crawling on all fours, succeeded in avoiding the second blow of one of the Indians.

"You're not going to be able to get away, goddamit!" Chiliquinga said, pursuing the cholo who was scurrying away like a lizard among the thickets in the ravine. When he caught up to him he dragged him by the rump and dealt him a well-aimed blow on the head, a blow which put Jacinto Quintana out of his misery forever.

"Now let's see you move, pes! You coward!"

Five corpses, including those of Jacinto Quintana and One-Eyed Rodríguez, were left lying along the mountain paths in that first skirmish which lasted until nightfall.

When the macabre news from the village, together with the shouts of the Indian throng—which grew in size with each passing minute—reached the hacienda, Mr. Chapy, who had been an illustrious guest at Cuchitambo for the past two weeks, slapped the landowner on the back and reminded him:

"You see, my dear friend, how you don't know where you're treading."

"Sí, but this is no time for jokes. Let's escape to Quito," Don Alfonso suggested with ill-disguised terror.

"Yes . . ."

"We'll have to send in an armed force. I'll speak with

my relatives and with the authorities. This affair can be settled only by bullets."

An automobile raced along the road at full speed, like a dog with its tail between its legs, as though in dread of the cry from the mountain which now was making the whole region tremble:

"Ñucanchic huasipungooo!!"

THE FOLLOWING MORNING the hacienda houses were attacked. When the Indians entered the main house they redoubled their shouts—shouts whose echoes resounded on the old doors with large wrought iron knockers, in the basement, in the abandoned oratory, in the spacious halls, in the shed where the oven was, and in the main stables. Unable to find the mayordomo, whom they would have gladly crushed, the huasipungueros freed the huasicamas and the pongos. Even though the granaries and the storerooms were empty, they found plenty of provisions in the pantry. Unfortunately, when their hunger was sated a superstitious fear spread over them, and they fled once more to the hill and to their huasipungos, still shouting the phrase that had infused them with rage, love and sacrifice:

"Ñucanchic huasipungooo!"

From the capital, with the swiftness with which government authorities act in these matters, two hundred infantrymen were sent to quell the rebellion. Among social and governmental circles the news was repeated with a liberal sprinkling of indignation and of heroic orders:

"Such bandits ought to be killed without mercy."

"Exterminate them like other civilized nations have already done."

"Get rid of them for the peace of our Christian homes."

"We must defend our national leaders . . . Defend Don Alfonso Pereira, who built a road all by himself."

"We must defend the unselfish and civilizing foreign businesses established on our soil."

The soldiers arrived in Tomachi led by a major, a hero of a hundred military revolts and as many counterrevolts, who, before getting down to his work, wet his whistle and drank in courage with a good dose of brandy at Juana's bar. Juana, at this time Quintana's widow, was exhausted and constantly crying during the preparations for her husband's wake.

"My dear general . . . My dear colonel . . . Just drink up. It'll make you stronger . . . Kill every single one of those villainous Indians . . . Just see how they made me a widow overnight."

"To your health . . . For you, good lady . . ."

"You're too kind. I only hope you catch a few of those Indians alive so we can really teach them a lesson."

"That's going to be hard to do. During the famous Indian uprising at Cuenca I tried to threaten them and ordered my soldiers to fire into the air. It was useless. I accomplished nothing."

"They're savages, that's all."

"We had to kill a lot of them. More than a hundred Indians."

"Here . . ."

"It'll be all over in about two hours."

By mid-afternoon the troops from the capital began the ascent of the hillside. The rifle and machine gun bullets partly silenced the shouts of the rebellious Indian throng. Military patrols, crawling forward to take cover in the bends, the ditches, and the gorges hunted down the Indians, their women and their children. The Indians, with the desperation of frightened rats, sought to hide, and crept into every possible refuge: the caves, the cat-tail growths in the swamps, the foliage of the chaparral, the fissures in the rocks, and the depths of the ravines.

At first it was easy for the soldiers, thanks to the panic which, wrought by the first volleys, very quickly brought down a good-sized group of the braver men. It was easy for them to advance fearlessly, sharpening their aim on the Indian women, on the children, and on the men who weren't able to retreat in an orderly fashion in order to continue their resistance.

"Look, cholo. There's one hiding in those bushes. He thinks . . ."

"You're right. I saw him."

"He's hiding from the patrol which is coming up the road."

"Just watch my shooting, goddamit!"

The shot rang out: a tall, lean Indian came out of the chaparral like a drunkard, clutched his hands to his chest, and tried to speak, or curse perhaps, but a second shot chopped down the Indian and all his good or bad words.

"Goddam! This is a cowardly thing to kill them just like this."

"And what else can we do pes? It's orders from our superiors."

"But they're unarmed."

"Armed or unarmed, the major said."

"Armed or unarmed . . ."

In another patrol which was advancing along the other side of the slope similar scenes and dialogues were taking place:

"The other one got away, goddamit. But this one won't escape me."

"The other one was just a child, pes. This one looks like an old Indian."

"It's hard to do it."

"Why should it be hard? You'll see, I . . ."

"Shoot him."

"You'll learn how. One shot right in the bread basket."

As an echo to the shot an anguished cry was heard and, with the corners of his poncho catching on the branches of the tree, the Indian who had been so skillfully hunted fell to the ground.

"Sonofabitch! I got him. With me there's no fooling around."

"But that Indian's cry went clear through me."

"That's just how it is at first. Later one gets used to it."

"One gets used to it."

Actually, the fury of conquest heightened the cruelty of the soldiers. They hunted down and killed the rebels with the same diligence, with the same amorality and dispatch with which they would have crushed some poisonous vermin. Let them all be killed! Yes. The small children who had sought protection with some women under the foliage which projected over the muddy waters of a pool also fell victims to the merciless blows of a hail of machine gun bullets.

With the afternoon almost gone, the sun, about to dive behind the western hills, crimsoned the clouds in a bloody reflection of the pools below. Only the Indians who had succeeded in falling back courageously toward Andrés Chiliquinga's huasipungo, which was protected by a steep, twisting path leading up to it and by precipices all around, still resisted, digging themselves into the advantageous terrain.

"We'll have to attack soon so that the Indians entrenched on the ridge won't escape during the night. The slope is steep but . . . ," the leader said to his soldiers impatiently. And without finishing the sentence, with a frog-like hop, he took cover in a hollow just in time to escape the charge of a huge boulder which rolled downhill leaping like an angry bull.

"Uuuy."

"Goddam!"

"Get out of there."

"If I didn't move just in the nick of time those Indian bastards would have smashed me," exclaimed an officer coming out of a ditch and glaring at the top of the hill, his eyes laden with hate and defiance.

"They must not get away. If the worst comes to the worst, they'll meet up with some Indians from the rest of the country and then we'll be involved in a real battle," said the major.

Sheltered in a ditch that opened a short distance from Chiliquinga's hut, a group of Indians, trembling with rage, hurled rocks down the slope. And one of them fired away with an old fowling-piece.

Suddenly the soldiers began to fan out and crawl up the slope, mounting a step at a time on the stairs carved out, one by one, by the bursts of machine gun fire. As the firing grew closer the imprudence of the Indian women who were bringing rocks, unsheltered by the ditch, left them stretched out on the slope forever.

"Goddam! Bring more rocks, pes!" shouted the entrenched Indians. But the only answer was a murmur of moans and ohs that dragged itself along the ground to reach their ears. All at once, tragic mystery, bayonets sprouted like sharp teeth along the lower lip of the ditch. Several Indians were skewered to the ground.

"This way, taiticu," Chiliquinga's son urged, pulling on his father's poncho and leading him through an opening into a small drainage ditch. Four other Indians who had heard the boy's invitation also escaped through the same opening. Crawling on all fours and led by the boy, they shortly reached the back of Andrés' hut and hurriedly entered it. Instinctively they blocked the door with everything they could: the stone to grind the grain, the fireplace bricks, the firewood, and timbers. The silence they felt outside, the walls, and the roof brought them the security of a sturdy shelter. They used the pause that ensued to wipe off their faces dirtied with sweat and dust, to grind out curses under their breath, and to scratch their heads. It was like waking up to a nightmare. Who had gotten them into such a mess? And why? They looked surreptitiously at Chiliquinga with the same superstitious and vengeful anguish with which they had approached the sheriff or One-Eyed Rodríguez just before they killed them. They glared at the Indian who had gathered them together with the diabolical witchcraft of his battle horn. "He . . . He was to blame, goddamit!" But serious and urgent matters were developing faster than their black suspicions and their evil intentions. The expectant silence was suddenly shattered in the interior of the hut. A blaze of machine gun fire riddled the thatch roof. Chiliquinga's son, who until that moment had instilled courage in the older Indians with his craftiness and helpful unconcern, cried out and clung trembling to his father's legs.

"Taiticu. Taiticu, help us, pes," he begged.

"You little Indian coward. Why are you crying now, pes? Just keep your mouth shut," muttered Chiliquinga, swallowing his curses and his tears of impotence while he sheltered his son with his arms and his tattered poncho.

The bursts of bullets quickly set fire to the straw roof. The timbers began to burn. Amid the asphyxiating smoke that filled the hovel—a black smoke of soot and of misery—amid the crying of the little one, amid the coughing that tore at everyone's chest and throat, amid the shower of hot embers from the roof, amid the stinging odors that basted their eyes, the curses and complaints spurted entreatingly:

"Goddam!"

"Taiticuuu. Something, do something, pes."

"We'll be roasted like guinea pigs."

"Like a soul in hell."

"Like the devil himself."

"Taiticu."

"Just open the door."

"Just open it, goddamit!"

Unable to think clearly because of the choking smoke and the sobbing of the boy, the Indians made Chiliquinga open the door which was beginning to burn at that moment. Behind them was the ravine, over their heads the fiery roof and before the flying bullets.

"Just open it, goddamit!"

"Oh, Goddam!"

"Sonofabitch!"

Andrés quickly removed the objects blocking the door, put his child under his arm, like a precious bundle, and opened the door.

"Go out, damn it! You cowards!"

The afternoon breeze refreshed his face. His eyes could again see life for a few short moments, feel it like

. . . something . . . "What the hell," he said to himself. He pressed the boy under his arm, ran out of the house, tried to curse, and shouted with a cry that pierced the fiercest rain of bullets:

"Ñucanchic huasipungo!"

Then he ran forward eager to drown out the stupid barks of the rifles. Shouting in unison with the others whom he felt behind him, he repeated:

"Ñucanchic huasipungo, goddamit!"

Suddenly, like a bolt of lightning, everything grew silent for him and for them. Soon after, too, the hut stopped burning. The sun sank definitively. Above the silence, above the strangled protest, the national flag of the glorious battalion fluttered with undulations of mocking laughter. And afterwards? The gringo gentlemen.

At dawn, up from the demolished huts, from the rubble, from the ashes, from the still warm corpses, as if in a dream, a crop of thin arms sprouted like spikes of barley. Strummed by the icy winds off the paramos of all the Americas they emitted a piercing screeching cry:

"Ñucanchic huasipungo!"

"Ñucanchic huasipungo!"

Glossary

The reader who knows no Spanish or Quechua (the Andean Indian tongue inherited from the Incas) should note the different manner of spelling the same words. For example, the Spanish word *amo* will be written correctly when pronounced by anyone but the Indians. But when the Indian says the same word, Icaza, faithful to the Indian accent, writes the word as *amu*. Thus, in many words which are correctly spelled with an "o" we will find a "u" when they are spoken by the Indian. In the glossary such words follow the Spanish spelling.

The only other difficulty in using the glossary may be the frequent use of the diminutive suffix on a Spanish word. There are two principal ways to show such a suffix in Spanish: with *ito* and with *ico*. For example, *socorros* means the yearly handout to the Indians. The Indian, wishing to show humbleness and to diminish the size of the handout, will often use the word *socorritus*. (Note that the final "o" has become a "u.") In the glossary we have indexed only the base word, *socorros*, except under the word *taita*. After *taita* we have listed *taiticu* and the doubly diminished *taitiquitu* along with their appropriate translations. Since the diminutive ending is often used to show affection as well as diminution the reader must select the proper meaning according to the context.

We thought it proper and even essential to maintain these words in the original tongues for without them a good deal of the Andean flavor of the original would be lost in the translation.

achachay	an exclamation expressing sensation of cold.
amo	owner; used by servants to refer to their master. The Indian often uses *amu* or *amitu* for *amo*.
arí	the Indian word for yes.
arrarray	an exclamation expressing a burning sensation.
arrayán	a hardwood; a variety of the myrtle tree.
ay	the standard Spanish expression for pain, grief or surprise.
beata	a very religious woman; used very often of one who has a false piety; hence a hypocrite.

bonito	good, beautiful. The Indian uses *bonitu*.
caca	vulgar name for excrement.
canela negra	a hardwood.
carajo	exclamation equivalent to goddam or sonofabitch.
chacracama	an Indian who watches the fields at night.
chamiza	firewood.
chasquibay	the lamentations of the family and close relatives before the cadaver.
chicha	alcoholic drink generally made of fermented corn.
chiguagua	a figure made of fireworks; usually in shape of a doll or of a human being.
chilca	a resinous bush with many straight thin branches with leaves like those of a willow tree. The leaves are used for medicinal purposes.
cholo	person of mixed Indian and white blood.
chugchi	the gleanings gathered in the fields after the crop has been harvested.
comadre	a very good friend, a close neighbor. (This word used only of women; the corresponding word for men is *compadre*.)
creciente	flood
cuiche (or *Cuichi*)	an evil spirit who inhabits the hills or ravines.
Cunshi	nickname for Spanish *Concepción*.
cura	a parish priest.
curandero -a	a quack doctor; in general, any person practicing medicine without having studied it.
Dios mío	heavens! (literally, my God!)
frailejones	plants with golden yellow flowers; they produce a resinous substance used in rural medicine.

ga	an expression used just to give emphasis to a phrase.
guagua	Indian word for a child, especially a baby not yet weaned.
guarapo	the fermented juice of the sugar cane. A drink often used by the Indians to achieve intoxication.
huasicama	an Indian caretaker of the manor house.
huasipungo	a parcel of land which the owner of the hacienda grants an Indian family in return for their daily labor. The Indian occupant wrests what he can from this piece of land and erects his miserable hovel on it.
huasipunguero	the Indian who lives on the *huasipungo* and is tied to any debt that has accrued on it.
huilmo	a hardwood.
jachimayshay	the Indian rite of bathing the dead to facilitate the corpse's voyage on to eternity.
junta	a meeting of persons to discuss a certain issue.
longo, -a	an Indian child or adolescent.
longuito, -a	diminutive of *longo;* often used to show affection.
mayordomo	an hacienda employee in charge of workmen and their labor.
minga	a collective labor often done by an entire village for no pay except the abundant food and plenty of at least one alcoholic beverage. Dates from Inca days.
minguero, -a	one who works on a *minga.*
motilón	a hardwood.
niña	in Spanish a girl or young woman. Indians use this word sometimes to refer to, or to show respect for any white woman.

ñucanchic huasipungo	the first word means "our"; thus the entire phrase may be freely translated as "Let's fight for our *huasipungos*."
paisano	a rustic; often used as "hick."
panza	a hardwood.
páramo	high, and cold, plateau.
pasillo	a popular dance melody.
patrón, -a	boss, master; *patrona* is feminine equivalent.
patrón grande, su merced	a lofty phrase denoting the elegant almost omnipotent position of the *patrón* vis-à-vis the Indians who work for him.
patroncitu	diminutive of *patrón*, often showing humility on the part of the Indian toward his master.
peón -(es)	peasant(s)
pes	a common contraction of the Spanish *pues*. Usually means "well," "now then," etc.
pongo	an Indian who works about the manor house without pay.
prioste	in Ecuador, the one who asks for, or accepts the financial responsibility for a religious feast day.
rosca	a scornful word for "Indian."
runa	an Indian.
sanjuanito	an Indian song and dance.
shunguitico	diminutive of *shungo*, affectionately used.
socorros	a yearly handout by the *patrón* which, together with the *huasipungo* and the *raya*—a nominal daily wage—make up the entire payment the Indian receives for his labor.
soroche	altitude sickness.
taita	papa, daddy. Used especially by the Indians and other rural inhabitants in the Andean regions.

Taita, Taita Dios	God, Almighty Father.
taiticu	diminutive of *taita*. Usually shows more affection or humility than *taita*.
taitiquitu	a diminutive of *taiticu!* (more humble than *taiticu*).
tapial	a wall usually enclosing country properties or homes.
uuuy	an exclamation.
viva	hoorah! hoorah for!